PRAISE FOR M. L. BUCHMAN

A fabulous soaring thriller.

— *TAKE OVER AT MIDNIGHT,* MIDWEST
BOOK REVIEW

Meticulously researched, hard-hitting, and suspenseful.

— *PURE HEAT,* PUBLISHERS WEEKLY,
STARRED REVIEW

Expert technical details abound, as do realistic military missions with superb imagery that will have readers feeling as if they are right there in the midst and on the edges of their seats.

— *LIGHT UP THE NIGHT,* RT REVIEWS, 4 1/2
STARS

Buchman has catapulted his way to the top tier of my favorite authors.

— FRESH FICTION

Nonstop action that will keep readers on the edge of their seats.

— TAKE OVER AT MIDNIGHT, LIBRARY JOURNAL

M L. Buchman's ability to keep the reader right in the middle of the action is amazing.

— LONG AND SHORT REVIEWS

The only thing you'll ask yourself is, "When does the next one come out?"

— WAIT UNTIL MIDNIGHT, RT REVIEWS, 4 STARS

The first...of (a) stellar, long-running (military) romantic suspense series.

— THE NIGHT IS MINE, BOOKLIST, "THE 20 BEST ROMANTIC SUSPENSE NOVELS: MODERN MASTERPIECES"

I knew the books would be good, but I didn't realize how good.

— NIGHT STALKERS SERIES, KIRKUS REVIEWS

Buchman mixes adrenalin-spiking battles and brusque military jargon with a sensitive approach.

— PUBLISHERS WEEKLY

13 times "Top Pick of the Month"

— NIGHT OWL REVIEWS

Tom Clancy fans open to a strong female lead will clamor for more.

— *DRONE*, PUBLISHERS WEEKLY

Superb! Miranda is utterly compelling!

— *BOOKLIST,* STARRED REVIEW

Miranda Chase continues to astound and charm.

— BARB M.

Escape Rating: A. Five Stars! OMG just start with *Drone* and be prepared for a fantastic binge-read!

— READING REALITY

The best military thriller I've read in a very long time. Love the female characters.

— *DRONE,* SHELDON MCARTHUR,
FOUNDER OF THE MYSTERY BOOKSTORE,
LA

DAMIEN'S CHRISTMAS

A NIGHT STALKERS HOLIDAY ROMANTIC SUSPENSE

M. L. BUCHMAN

Other works by M. L. Buchman: *(* - also in audio)*

Action-Adventure Thrillers

Dead Chef
One Chef!
Two Chef!

Miranda Chase
Drone*
Thunderbolt*
Condor*
Ghostrider*
Raider*
Chinook*
Havoc*
White Top*
Start the Chase*

Science Fiction / Fantasy

Deities Anonymous
Cookbook from Hell: Reheated
Saviors 101

Single Titles
Monk's Maze
the Me and Elsie Chronicles

Contemporary Romance

Eagle Cove
Return to Eagle Cove
Recipe for Eagle Cove
Longing for Eagle Cove
Keepsake for Eagle Cove

Love Abroad
Heart of the Cotswolds: England
Path of Love: Cinque Terre, Italy

Where Dreams
Where Dreams are Born
Where Dreams Reside
Where Dreams Are of Christmas*
Where Dreams Unfold
Where Dreams Are Written
Where Dreams Continue

Non-Fiction

Strategies for Success
Managing Your Inner Artist/Writer
Estate Planning for Authors*
Character Voice
Narrate and Record Your Own
Audiobook*

Short Story Series by M. L. Buchman:

Action-Adventure Thrillers

Dead Chef

Miranda Chase Origin Stories

Romantic Suspense

Antarctic Ice Fliers

US Coast Guard

Contemporary Romance

Eagle Cove

Other

Deities Anonymous (fantasy)

Single Titles

The Emily Beale Universe
(military romantic suspense)

The Night Stalkers
MAIN FLIGHT
The Night Is Mine
I Own the Dawn
Wait Until Dark
Take Over at Midnight
Light Up the Night
Bring On the Dusk
By Break of Day
Target of the Heart
Target Lock on Love
Target of Mine
Target of One's Own
NIGHT STALKERS HOLIDAYS
Daniel's Christmas*
Frank's Independence Day*
Peter's Christmas*
Christmas at Steel Beach
Zachary's Christmas*
Roy's Independence Day*
Damien's Christmas*
Christmas at Peleliu Cove

Henderson's Ranch
Nathan's Big Sky*
Big Sky, Loyal Heart*
Big Sky Dog Whisperer*
Tales of Henderson's Ranch*

Shadow Force: Psi
At the Slightest Sound*
At the Quietest Word*
At the Merest Glance*
At the Clearest Sensation*

White House Protection Force
Off the Leash*
On Your Mark*
In the Weeds*

Firehawks
Pure Heat
Full Blaze
Hot Point*
Flash of Fire*
Wild Fire
SMOKEJUMPERS
Wildfire at Dawn*
Wildfire at Larch Creek*
Wildfire on the Skagit*

Delta Force
Target Engaged*
Heart Strike*
Wild Justice*
Midnight Trust*

Emily Beale Universe Short Story Series
The Night Stalkers
The Night Stalkers Stories
The Night Stalkers CSAR
The Night Stalkers Wedding Stories
The Future Night Stalkers

Delta Force
Th Delta Force Shooters
The Delta Force Warriors

Firehawks
The Firehawks Lookouts
The Firehawks Hotshots
The Firebirds

White House Protection Force
Stories

Future Night Stalkers
Stories (Science Fiction)

The Emily Beale Universe
Reading Order Road Map

any series and any novel may be read stand-alone
(all have a complete heartwarming Happy Ever After)

The Emily Beale Universe

The Night Stalkers
(#1 *The Night Is Mine*)

The Night Stalkers
5D, 5E & CSAR
Stories

Night Stalkers
Holidays

Delta Force

Firehawks

Henderson's
Ranch

Delta Force
Stories

Smokejumpers

White House
Protection Force

ShadowForce
PSI

Fire Lookouts,
Hotshots,
& Firebirds
Stories

Dilya's
Dog Force*

WHPF
Stories

The Future
Night Stalkers
Stories

* *Coming soon*

For more information and alternate reading orders, please
visit: www.mlbuchman.com/reading-order

ABOUT THIS BOOK

A Christmas message—warning of the next big attack on US soil—needs the comfort of a pastrami on rye.

"Top Pick of the Month" – Night Owl Reviews

Cornelia Day, still overwhelmed by her first week as the new Presidential Chief of Staff, needs help and she needs it fast.

Damien Feinman leads the Situation Room management team. He is definitely falling for the frosty Cornelia Day. And he absolutely needs a pastrami sandwich from Katz's Deli to make it through the holidays.

When a Christmas message from an unfriendly foreign power warns of destruction, only together can Damien and Cornelia unravel the message before it becomes lethal.

[Can be read stand-alone or in series. A complete happy-ever-after with no cliffhangers. Originally published in "The Night Stalkers White House" series in 2016. Re-edited 2022 for improved reader experience but still the same great story.]

1

STANDING ON THE THRESHOLD OF THE WHITE HOUSE Situation Room shouldn't be this strange, but Cornelia could not remember a single moment of greater change in her life.

Taking the next step seemed beyond her capabilities.

And it wasn't merely the Situation Room—which was actually a large complex of rooms in the basement of the West Wing. This was the entry to the President's Briefing Room, the keystone conference room. This is where the nation's hardest decisions were made and she absolutely didn't belong here.

"Well, here's a day I never thought I'd see," President-elect Zachary Thomas chuckled from close behind her. "The day anything would slow down Ms. Cornelia Day."

Fighting to keep her reactions to herself, she took the step, and the next five, her heels echoing as she crossed the pale gold marble and then onto the dark blue of the carpet surrounding the conference table.

In her eight years as Vice President Thomas' assistant, she had never entered this room.

Didn't he know that?

The dark walnut table had six armchairs down either side. At the near end was the lone chair that must be the President's and at the far end there was a wall of video screens. More chairs lined either sidewall as well as more large screens.

The room felt wrong, too simple for what it was. The governor's conference room in Colorado was several times larger and much more nicely appointed. Of course the Roosevelt Room and Cabinet Room upstairs were directly opposite the Oval Office.

But *still*, the Situation Room should look like more than an afterthought. It was so small for what happened here. If all the chairs were filled it would be more cramped than the coach section on an airplane.

Then she looked at the clock. Local time and—she barely managed a breath against the tightness building in her chest—President time. He had his own clock. Nothing so succinctly stated the purpose of this room as him having his own clock. It would always be synchronized to where he traveled in the world.

She *truly* didn't belong here. She didn't even know which chair would be hers, or more troubling, why it would be hers.

"This," Zachary Thomas came up beside her and rested his hand on the head chair, "will typically be mine starting on Inauguration Day."

It was the Monday after Thanksgiving. They had barely seven weeks to form their new administration. Cornelia's head hurt from thinking about how much there was to do.

"And if you don't think that's scaring the daylights out of me, you've got another think coming. That one," he pointed to his immediate left, the chair she'd stopped close behind, "is where my White House Chief of Staff will be sitting."

Cornelia rested her hand on the seat back and tried not to be physically ill. At the President of the United States' left hand. "How did this happen?"

"Cornelia."

She managed to look up at his dark eyes.

"It happened because I need someone to keep me from screwing the pooch...too often. You've been with me since before I was the Governor of Colorado, almost a dozen years. You know me better than anyone, even Anne."

Cornelia doubted that. First Lady-elect Anne Darlington-Thomas had shown a heartfelt understanding of her future husband since the day they'd met last Christmas—an affinity that neither Cornelia, nor Anne had expected. But Cornelia wasn't comfortable correcting the President-elect on her first-ever visit to the Situation Room.

"There hasn't been a policy decision in all those years that you didn't offer something on."

"Even when I disagreed with you," she managed a smile.

"Especially when you disagreed with me. You know how many people are willing to speak *truth* to the Governor, never mind the President? I need someone who will."

"I can't believe you did this to me, Mr. President-elect!" Daniel Darlington strode into the Situation Room.

His hearty greeting echoed Cornelia's sentiments exactly.

"Hey!" Daniel aimed a finger at the chair her hand rested on. "That's my chair!"

Cornelia snatched her hand back.

"Nope," Zachary pointed to his right. "*That's* going to be yours very soon, Daniel."

"I can *not* believe you conned me into this," Daniel

repeated but he moved to the designated chair and dropped into it as if there was nothing unusual.

It fit him.

With his immaculate suit, surfer blond hair, and charming smile, Daniel was one of the most politically savvy people, and well-liked ones, in DC. He had proven he was an exceptional White House Chief of Staff and she had no doubt that he'd make an amazing Vice President.

"I'm supposed to be back on the family farm in two months. Remind me again how you convinced me to run with you?"

"I asked and you said yes. You didn't even whine much," Zachary sat in his own future chair at the head of the table. Cornelia wished he'd at least squirm a little as he did, so that she wasn't the only one so obviously out of place.

"And I expect to regret it for the rest of my days. But my wife said she'd vote for me, so I caved. Sorry Mr. President-elect, but you're not the one Alice voted for on our ticket."

"Likely story."

The two men shared smiles that told Cornelia this was going to be her life for the next four to eight years. They were both simply too pleased with themselves and each other. It didn't help that, through Anne, they were also now brothers-in-law.

Cornelia was halfway into her seat when Daniel aimed that charming smile at her.

"Careful. If this all goes wrong, you'll be the one in the Vice President's chair eight years from now. Four if I have the good sense to quit while I'm ahead."

She collapsed into her seat with far less dignity than she'd intended. She straightened both her spine and the line of her best Ann Thomas suit to regain her composure before replying.

"I will change my citizenship tomorrow," she said with all of the aplomb she could muster.

"Aruba's a good choice," Daniel suggested with a casual ease that unraveled her attempts to set a tone befitting the White House Situation Room.

"I'd go with Australia," Zachary riposted. "Better beer."

Cornelia sighed. They were here for their first Sit Room briefing as the incoming administration. And if this was any indicator for how their schedule was going to go over the next four years (never mind if there were *two* terms) she would go insane managing it.

Except that wouldn't be her job anymore.

President Zachary Thomas would have a body man and a fleet of secretaries. Her job would be about managing his information flow, not his hour-to-hour schedule.

Definitely time to up your game, Cornelia.

"Personally," a new voice sounded from behind her, "I prefer German beer. There is a beer called Rieder Dunkle Weisse—dark white—in Bavaria. Very traditional, very local. It does not ship well and should only be drunk in Munich and only in the fall. However, considering the next five-year projection for regional stability, I would not recommend an actual citizenship change to Germany at this time, Ms. Day, nor Aruba. However, I must say that I think that chair fits you very well."

Cornelia could only look at the man aghast. Everything they'd said in one of the most secure rooms in the world and —none of it was private. She wouldn't forget that lesson soon. Which, of course, was the point of the newcomer's lesson.

The tall, dark-haired man looked vaguely professorial in a slightly rumpled suit. But in contrast his bearing and broad shoulders said military, or perhaps ex-military as he didn't display the expected rigidity. His New York accent went well with the slightly pompous tone of his thinking he was the smartest one in the room.

———

DAMIEN FEINMAN ALWAYS ENJOYED THIS MOMENT, THOUGH HE knew it was no surprise to the Gentlemen Elect. He considered this to be one of the perks of being head of the Situation Room duty watch.

Every word said in the Briefing Room was overheard by the room's National Security Council watch officers. This allowed the occupants to simply ask for any data and his watch would provide—one of their many duties. He'd always felt that a direct demonstration was the most effective on that point, which was very evident by Ms. Day's chagrined expression.

Damien had studied her file and was still scratching his head over it. Valedictorian at Claremont McKenna in three years, unheard of at that college. The debate team had won at the national level and been top three internationally for all three years she was on it—the last year as president. Straight to the Colorado Governor's office.

Everyone in Washington had assumed that Governor and then Vice President Zachary Thomas was dallying with her on the side. However, shortly before he began his run for President, Zachary Thomas had married Anne Darlington—and Cornelia Day had stood as maid-of-honor.

If she wasn't with the President-elect on the sly, then the intelligence indicated that she had even less of a life than he himself did.

However, Ms. Day in person was a very different woman than the one in her file. One look at her upright bearing made it impossible to imagine her doing a single improper thing. She sat like a dancer—her posture Audrey Hepburn perfect.

She stood to greet him. No, she *rose* to greet him; she even moved like a dancer. He'd had the hots for a girl in high school, for what little good it had done him, who went on to dance for the American Ballet Theatre. Ms. Day's simple rising from her chair was more graceful than Jara's dancing had been. Her merest movement made his breath catch in his throat.

The Elects offered him friendly smiles and handshakes which was kind of them. Ms. Day followed suit. She stood six-one in her two-inch heels. Her long fingers were as slender and fine as she was. There was an elegance to her that had nothing to do with her finely tailored suit. Unadorned right down to her unpainted nails except for a simple gold necklace chain. Her face was as slender as her body. Her straight fall of dark brown hair was immaculately sliced at shoulder length and swung back and forth with the neat precision of a knife at her cautious nod of greeting.

"I'm Marine Corps Captain Damien Feinman. Situation Room, senior duty watch officer."

"Cornelia Day," her tone polite, but cautious. Using only the five syllables of her own name she managed to accuse him of intruding and his listening in to be unwelcome.

It was easy to see why she'd picked up the nickname *The Shark*. Insanely intelligent, lean, and apparently lethal to anyone getting in the Vice President's way. Damien had heard rumors that congressmen would rather face Zachary Thomas than his assistant on any day of the week.

Dangerous and, the one thing that the file communicated least of all, beautiful. She was the killer combo.

And ten gets you twenty, Damien, she's as chilly on the inside as her reputation on the outside.

"I'm one of the National Security Council duty watch officers in charge of the Situation Room," he moved to the chair beside Daniel so that he could look at her across the table for the briefing.

No normal human had a file of her caliber and he wanted to unravel the puzzle of what data was missing. He liked puzzles and the woman across from him presented a fine one. He hoped the mystery wasn't too simple to solve— so many people had only a few layers to their truth.

Even the President-elect and the Vice-President-elect were not complicated men. Skilled, absolutely. Complicated? Both were moderately predictable, straightforward alpha males mitigated by a solid layer of decency and good upbringing.

"So, your job is to listen," Cornelia still sounded somewhat indignant about that, but was covering it well.

"To listen and to provide. This room is manned..." he paused a beat to tease the two women currently on the watch desk, "...or perhaps I should say peopled twenty-four hours a day by a minimum staff of five personnel. Three duty officers, a communications specialist, and an intelligence analyst."

"And which are you?" Cornelia's tone said she wasn't going to cut him a single inch of slack this side of Christmas.

"He," Zachary said, "is our friendly, neighborhood anomaly."

"We keep trying to straighten him out, but it doesn't do any good," Daniel agreed.

"Details on Ms. Day," he spoke loudly into the room and watched her for a reaction, then cursed under his breath. He should have changed the order of the presentation. If she was already offended, this was going to make things worse, but it was too late.

The screens beyond the end of the table flashed to life. Pictures from kindergarten through the recent election day rotating on one screen and an extensive bio on the other. He didn't bother to turn to read it, having memorized the key points. Instead he watched her, but her expression revealed nothing.

"Parents divorced. Mother a senior-level Raytheon engineer and father a high-school math teacher, the latter recently incarcerated because he did that thing with a female under-age student that you aren't supposed to do." Crap! Now he was sounding like an asshole starting on the most personal point. But he'd wanted to poke at that chilly facade; couldn't resist doing so.

"Does your precious file also indicate that I have neither seen nor heard from him since I was three? Not child support, not a birthday card, or Christmas present?"

It hadn't.

Her tone was absolutely flat, impossible to read hurt or pride into—*Just the facts, ma'am.* No wonder she scared the crap out of congressmen and senators alike; the woman was unreadable.

He typically started with the most personal information as a test. Most were shocked, dismayed, put off, even angered at the volume of information he had at his fingertips. Cornelia was calm and made it sound as if she was questioning his own intelligence for choosing such a starting point.

There was more shock from Zachary Thomas, who had employed her for over a decade, than there was from her. That degree of composure was unique in his experience. More rather than less intriguing on his puzzle scale.

"Merely an example of the types of information we can supply." He dismissed the rest of her file with a spoken word and spent the next twenty minutes giving the room's three occupants a rundown of the capabilities of the Situation Room and its staff. "With the Gentlemen Elect—"

"Gentlemen Elect?" Ms. Day asked as if that was the surprise.

"I rather prefer it to Messrs as the plural of Mister. Messrs Elect sounds as if they're preparing to make a mess."

Her nod for him to continue stated that she wouldn't be arguing the point, or perhaps not surprised if they did make one.

"With the Gentlemen Elect," he started over, "both in the top tier of the current administration, there is no need to compartmentalize information during this briefing." He'd been given authorization by the President that Ms. Day was also to be brought fully up to speed rather than awaiting Inauguration Day and her shift into the role of Chief of Staff.

For the Gentlemen Elect this was old news.

And it seemed no matter how fast he fed the information to her, Cornelia Day absorbed and cataloged it all. He wondered if it was a facade or if somehow her mind really was so quick and orderly that she could indeed remember the NSC staff's capabilities when she would have need of it.

He finished and waited, watching her.

Her smile was infinitesimal.

The cordovan-red leather portfolio—as slim as she was—that she had set on the table when she'd sat down had remained untouched, unopened. Now she reached out with her slender fingers, but merely turned it slightly so that its edge aligned more precisely with the table's.

Damien was fascinated. He'd seen plenty of men and a few women sit about this table over the years. A person, of either gender, that he couldn't read rated as either a cyborg or zombie—at least on the inside. That tiny smile gave her away as being neither.

Completely intrigued, he waited for what came next.

"You, Mr. Feinman," she inspected him with those dark brown eyes of hers. Was there a hidden laugh behind that thin smile? "Never answered my question."

Damien puzzled at that as her smile grew. *What question?*

He burst out laughing as he remembered and slapped the table: *What was he indeed!*

The Gentlemen Elect were looking at him as if he'd lost his mind.

He supposed that it was rude to laugh in the face of the next Commander in Chief, but was unable to help himself.

Both Zachary and Daniel chuckled along with him, but it was tentative. They didn't get it.

Only the woman across the table truly understood the joke and, while she didn't laugh, her smile went completely radiant—doubly so for how unexpected it was on her serious face.

Damien, still fighting for composure, rose to his feet and bowed deeply. It felt more like the curtain call at the end of *No, No, Nanette* in high school—in which he had played Jimmy the cheerful philanderer and, ironically for a Brooklyn Jew, wealthy Bible salesman.

"As to what I am, my good Ms. Day," he had to fight down the laugh. "I am the *intelligent* officer..."

Which almost earned him her laugh but not quite.

"But mostly—"

———

"HE'S THE LIBRARIAN."

Cornelia twisted about to see National Security Advisor Sienna Arnson stride into the room, her long red hair fiery bright and her shapely figure looking great in a Diane von Furstenberg dress. A woman who wore bright summer colors at the beginning of the DC winter and could somehow make it work. Cornelia's own charcoal slacks and jacket seemed dowdy beside the NSA.

Sienna sat in the chair beside Cornelia and directly across from Damien. But Sienna's answer did little to explain the man.

"You're...what?" Librarian was about the last title Cornelia would have expected.

Damien sighed for his stolen thunder and dropped back into his seat.

"You lack," she resisted the urge to ask if he bought his suits at Sears, "the military snap and precision I would expect from a handsome Marine Corps Captain. Now I understand why." And she should *not* have said handsome even if it was undeniable.

"Story of my life," Damien agreed and scowled at Sienna. Then he turned to Cornelia but raised his voice. "Story of my life, please."

In moments the briefing screens were filled with an array of images: high school photo, looking sharp in Marine blues complete with gold buttons, white hat, and sword. Damien Feinman looked good in his present suit whatever its origin, but he was remarkable in his dress uniform.

She scanned the biographic feed. High school drama department. Library school and Naval ROTC—odd combination. He was two months younger than she was— selfless Pisces to her own overly determined Capricorn.

Marine Corps intelligence at Quantico for two years. Ten years at—

"I thought National Security Council assignments to the White House Situation Room were only for two-year tours."

"That's why he's our anomaly," Zachary repeated his earlier statement.

But Damien wasn't looking at Zachary or at her. He was looking at the screens.

Cornelia followed the direction of his gaze and sighed. She didn't have an eidetic memory; no photograph of the information existed in her head—there was far too much of it. But she was *very* good at picking out what didn't fit in an array of information.

Many people, especially those subjected to her occasional in-vain attempts at relationships, found her ability disconcerting. She could see him wondering how she had zeroed in on his unexpected term of service here so quickly, it wasn't marked in any particular way to make it stand out in a busy display.

She read more during his puzzled silence. He too had been valedictorian and his climb through the ranks had been at a pace even combat officers rarely achieved. Clearly he too rose to a challenge.

"Now that you know how this place works," Sienna spoke up, "let's get into our first current affairs briefing. Until now, your intel briefings have been background material and longer term issues. As the others are already up to speed on world affairs, please let me know if I'm going too fast for you, Ms. Day. Starting with Africa."

The screens shifted again, but Cornelia wasn't watching them.

She was watching Damien Feinman as he slowly turned from the summary of his life to look at her. He was inspecting her carefully as if she was of sudden interest. They each had their skills, was it now a *contest* to see whose were more useful?

Cornelia arched a single eyebrow to voice the challenge and he offered a nod reminiscent of his mock bow to accept it.

Game on.

2

CORNELIA DIDN'T KNOW WHY SHE WAS ALWAYS FELT A JOLT OF surprise whenever she saw the President in the White House, and yet she did every single time. Over the last two terms, she'd had very little to do with President Matthews. Her primary contacts were with his three executive secretaries and Daniel; the President himself she never interacted with. He probably didn't know who she was.

At the end of the Sienna's hour-long briefing on the world at large, but before the meeting could break up, President Peter Matthews swept into the room.

"All rise," Damien called out like a court bailiff. He sent her a saucy wink. Then he snapped a Marine-smart salute to the President. "Good morning O Commander in Chief, my Commander."

"Sit down before you fall down, Feinman," was the President's easy greeting.

Damien remained standing respectfully despite his outrageous welcome.

Cornelia was fascinated by the various reactions as everyone rose to their feet. Zachary and Daniel became noticeably more casual in their speech—also offering cheery, even teasing greetings to the Commander in Chief— yet much more formal in their manner. Ties were surreptitiously straightened, jackets that had been over the backs of chairs were hurriedly donned. Sienna Arnson smoothed her dress carefully. She herself had neither shed her jacket nor fussed with the kerchief in her breast pocket that matched her blouse. She simply rose quietly and waited.

Damien, who had seemed unable to sit still during the course of the meeting, had slowly discombobulated himself. His tie had been eased, off center. He'd run his hands deep into his hair while trying to make a point, leaving it thoroughly mussed. His jacket had been left back at the watch stations from when he'd gone off to assist with items that were challenging the rest of the staff. His shirt sleeves were rolled up unevenly.

"Did I miss the surprise part yet?" President Matthews was immaculate in his three-piece pinstripe.

Zachary and Daniel exchanged looks, not of complicity but rather of confusion.

"The surprise part?" Sienna asked uncertainly.

Damien was keeping his thoughts to himself and Cornelia chose to emulate his example.

"Oh, did I forget to tell *anyone?*" President Matthews looked very pleased with himself as he sat in the chair that Zachary had occupied during the meeting. "Not yet, Cowboy. Move down one."

"That would be Flyboy. I'm from the Air Force Academy, not the flatlands of Colorado and you know it." Zachary moved to Daniel's chair and Daniel to Damien's.

Damien, rather than taking the next chair, circled around the other end of the table.

"What?" the President asked him.

"Boys on one side, girls on the other. Seems rather trite." Cornelia was amused as Damien scooted Sienna down one seat and sat between them.

"Ms. Day," the President said courteously, proving that he did indeed know who she was.

Realizing that she was the lone person still standing, she too returned to her seat.

"First," he turned to his right, "how far are you two into your transition team?"

Zachary and Daniel exchanged worried looks.

"They," Cornelia used the term loosely, "have filled under two hundred of one-thousand-forty-two open positions," and Cornelia had made most of those decisions herself because her boss had been too busy catching up with his Vice Presidential job since the election.

"When did that happen?" The President-elect did a poor job of covering for himself, as usual.

Cornelia kept her sigh to herself, but could hear Damien chuckle.

"That explains the steady stream of intelligence and personnel-clearance requests we've been processing lately."

She turned, a little startled at how close he suddenly was, seated in the next chair beside her.

"I've only told you part of what we do here. Those requests cross our desks as well. Never dull here, I can promise you."

She'd remember that.

"You two geniuses," the President addressed the Gentlemen Elect, she rather liked Damien's phrase, "do have the good sense to keep Sienna as National Security Advisor, don't you?"

Again Zachary and Daniel exchanged quick glances.

Cornelia read the look and made a mental note. "I'll get that taken care of. Congratulations, Ms. Arnson."

Sienna looked slightly dazed for a moment. "When they hadn't approached me, I'd assumed—"

"That they were still too dazzled about winning the election to think clearly, even though four weeks have passed by since?" Cornelia finished the sentence for her.

"Yes, that's it exactly. The answer is yes, by the way, once they get around to asking me. I'll cancel the feelers I put out to other agencies."

"Good," the President thumped a hand on the table, cutting off Zachary the moment he opened his mouth to actually ask.

Cornelia was starting to enjoy this. The President- and Vice-President-elect were both so confident; she'd have to remember the advantages of keeping them off balance.

"You two," the President continued, not giving them a chance to speak, "have an administration to prepare. You need to stop thinking about my lame duck operation and get moving."

"But—" Daniel didn't get past the first word of his protest before the President turned to her.

"You, Ms. Cornelia Day, are as of this moment, my White House Chief of Staff. Sorry Daniel, but that means I'll need your formal resignation by end of day unless you want me to fire your butt."

"I serve at the pleasure of the President," Daniel said it formally.

She could see him swallow hard. By his bewildered expression, it was going to take him a while to come to terms with the change. For herself, she simply filed the fact for later consideration.

No, there wasn't even the need for that. It made absolutely logical sense.

Her taking over now would smooth the often rough and occasionally acrimonious transition from one administration to the next. By naming her his White House Chief of Staff, President Matthews was showing a great deal of consideration for the incoming leadership.

"I'll leave it to the two of you when to switch offices but, Daniel and Zachary, make it soon—as in today. You two need to focus on the next administration. Cornelia, go to Daniel when you get stuck, but with your reputation I don't expect that to happen very often."

Again, more knowledge of her than she expected, but she had sufficient self-awareness to think that she had at least some skills at her job. If not, she never would have agreed to it when Zachary had swung by her office on Election Day and said, *Of course, if I win, you're my Chief of Staff. You know that, right?* Not waiting for her answer before rushing off to his next media event.

"Ms. Day, you should be able to get much more done now that you have the power of your future job. That's effective immediately, Damien." The President pulled a folded piece of paper out of his jacket's inner pocket and handed it over to him.

Cornelia took the liberty of reading the letter over Damien's shoulder to see that the President had already formalized her transition to his Chief of Staff.

Damien nodded his assent. When he attempted to return the letter, the President indicated that it should go to her.

Right. It would now be her responsibility to make sure it was properly filed. Whatever that meant.

The President rose and they all scrambled to do the same.

He shook her hand, actually taking hers between both of his as if to solemnize the moment.

"Best of luck! You're going to need it to survive these two." He nodded at Zachary and Daniel then departed without shaking their partially extended hands, but wearing a big smile. They were all such men.

The meeting ended. Mr. President- and Mr. Vice-President-elect were already deep in consultation regarding next steps on setting up their administration as they left the room.

Sienna still looked a little dazed as she followed in their wake.

Cornelia finally managed to unlock her knees and sit back down.

"I serve at the pleasure of the President," she whispered it to herself.

"That was a hell of a kicker, wasn't it, Ms. Day?" Damien asked from so close beside her that she jolted. "Sorry, guess you forgot that I was still here. A lot happening I know. No problem, we duty officers are used to being invisible."

When he started to rise, she rested a hand on his arm to keep him in place.

He waited her out while she sorted out her jumbled thoughts. She knew exactly who she wanted to keep and not keep from the current administration. The list formed rapidly in her head. And now she could take immediate action on building her own team: speechwriters, assistant chief of staff, press relations... The list wasn't endless, and thankfully it no longer felt that way. She also had a long list of appointments that she expected Zachary Thomas would sign off on with few changes, as soon as she double checked a few of them with—

She turned to Damien who was still eyeing her hand resting on his arm.

———

THE NEW WHITE HOUSE CHIEF OF STAFF CAUGHT HIM studying her hand.

Her file had said no attachments, other than the now dismissed possibility of one with the President-elect, and her ringless fingers were only a confirmation of that. It was ridiculous, but he liked the look of her hands. Fine but not delicate. He was—clearly losing his mind.

"Many Chiefs of Staff," Damien told her so that he'd have something to fill the sudden silence, "make the Situation Room into their second office." Was he being overly forward in hoping that this one would as well? She was yet another White House Chief of Staff, after all, and he'd seen six of those in his ten years here. She would only be Number Seven, nothing more. Yet it wasn't that simple. Was he such a cad that her gender was leading him to inappropriate preferences?

Cornelia finally withdrew her hand as if freeing him to rise and go.

If they had wild horses in DC, they weren't going to drag him away. But he couldn't think of any reason to stay beside her either. Thankfully, she spoke before good manners would make him attempt to stand once more.

"Perhaps," the surprise was gone from her voice at her sudden promotion.

Over the last few minutes, somewhere in that curious

mind of hers, she had either set aside or fully integrated her changed role into her identity—and he'd bet on the latter.

"You could take a moment to explain the implications of my new role from your perspective."

It was a very smart question. He had learned during the course of the briefing that it was the only kind she asked.

As he did explain, she began to relax. Not her breathtaking posture, but now removed from the powerhouse personalities of the country's leaders, she began asking more questions. It had been hard to calibrate her silences during the earlier meetings. Her rare questions hadn't provided sufficient reference.

He finally pieced together what was missing: Cornelia Day was shy. He'd never have expected that of her, but the more they spoke, the more true it seemed. But shyness had nothing to do with intelligence.

Whenever Damien had to instruct new staff, he always worked to find their level of knowledge first and then teach them starting at that level. Once it was only the two of them, he found Cornelia Day's level easily enough—higher than he'd thought despite reading her file then sitting across from her these last two hours.

But the more he described the NSC's capabilities, the more insightful her questions became until she was nearly speaking on Daniel's level—and he'd been Chief of Staff for seven years.

"Well, that's the gist of it," he finally ground to a halt. Still she hadn't taken a single note.

She nodded, and glanced at the wall clock as if she'd been in the room enough times for it to become habit. Not at her wrist—she didn't wear a watch. No instinctive reaching for her phone—which had been confiscated at the

Sit Room's entrance to avoid unauthorized calls, photos, or recordings.

"Past one," he noted. "How do you feel about lunch?"

"It depends," she looked at him without blinking as if she was going to hypnotize him.

"On?"

"On whether or not you're going to answer my question."

It wasn't enough for her that he was head of the duty watch. She was now asking the next level question of who he was that he had retained a position for ten years that none held for more than two.

He could get to truly like this woman.

———

"I RARELY EAT HERE," CORNELIA TOLD DAMIEN WHILE THE waiter eased in her blue leather chair as she sat down. The wood-paneled walls of the Navy Mess in the basement of the White House were adorned with large paintings of the Navy's ships dating from when the national fleet moved only by sea and wind.

"Where do you usually eat? *Do* you usually eat?" Damien's nod to her slender body was frank and easy-going.

She'd heard that one often enough. Her metabolism burned calories at an alarming rate. Missing a meal could set her into a lightheaded tailspin if she wasn't careful.

He'd recovered his jacket, but his tie was still in disarray and she resisted the urge to straighten it. He dropped into his chair and hopped it toward the table, pinching his hand between chair arm and the underside of the table with a silverware-rattling bang.

"I typically opt for a sandwich at my desk or a takeout

salad from a nearby coffee shop when I'm working at the Vice President's office in the Eisenhower Executive Office Building." The VP's only staff space in the White House was an office with an assistant's outer office—which until an hour ago had been her exclusive domain for eight years.

Damien looked around critically, "I actually can't remember the last time I ate here. My shift allows little time for breaks."

"And yet today, here you are."

He turned his attention fully back upon her. His gaze locked on with such a force as to be palpable. "And yet today, here I am."

She almost asked after the occasion, hoping for a different answer than she suddenly expected, and then decided against it. It was one of those moments that was either to curry her favor because she had easy access to President-elect Zachary Thomas, or it was because...she sighed to herself. Why did men always treat her like a woman rather than a person?

"A chance to dine with..." he offered a friendly smile, warning her all too well that his next words would be *such a beautiful*—"...the new Chief of Staff."

Not quite what she expected, making her glad she'd internalized her sigh.

Very glad actually. Having spent most of the morning with Damien, she was rather enjoying his company. He lacked the hard DC edge that so many people acquired here. At times she was afraid that she had acquired that edge as well, and past all recovery.

"You have an unanswered question," he showed enough wisdom to change the topic. "I'm a fourth generation librarian on one side and a third generation Marine on the other."

He waited, but she didn't know for what. For her to step into the middle of some assumption? Instead, she ordered the chicken fajita salad and a glass of caffeine-free Diet Coke—she needed neither high, chemical nor sugar—and kept her silence. That appeared to amuse him as he ordered a burger and a root beer.

"My great-great-grandfather on my father's side was one of Carnegie's first librarians right here in DC."

"That would be five generations."

"My grandfather was a black sheep and made his living as an insurance salesman. No one can account for him, least of all my grandmother."

"That makes you a Marine on your mother's side?"

"It does. Grandma was in the Marine Corps during Vietnam through Desert Storm—clerical work. Mom served in a somewhat more enlightened age and is still an MV-22 Osprey pilot—though she's a stateside trainer now."

"Which explains what about you?" Actually it told her a great deal—high intelligence, deep motivation, and an unusual view of the world. But she wanted to know what conclusions it had given him.

"As the first one to combine the two professions, it has given me an immense respect for strong women." This time his nod to her communicated precisely that.

Cornelia wasn't quite sure what to do with the sudden warmth inside her. People always saw her as a political player without being a woman at all, or as a woman who could only possibly be interested in marrying well in Washington no matter how often she proved otherwise.

Each election cycle she had to deal with all of the freshman senators and congressmen coming to meet the Vice President and thinking they were God's gift to his *lonely* assistant. The offers had redoubled with his marriage this spring when it became clear that the rumors about them having a romantic connection were untrue. She'd tried wearing a ring for a while, but that had only served to increase the seediness of the propositions.

She wondered if Damien was the first person to see her as both woman and political player at once. Her mother certainly didn't. All she saw was a daughter she loved but didn't begin to understand.

The setting of the Navy Mess in the White House basement was beautiful, the food excellent, and the company...exceptional. The conversation ranged widely across literature, politics, and his mother's service experience as a female Marine.

It was only after she was climbing the stairs alone to the first floor that she realized that Damien had still managed to avoid answering her question of why he was the long-serving *anomaly*, though she no longer thought it was intentional. Or perhaps he had answered. His intelligence and clear insights placed him sufficiently above any norm that his remaining in the position made sense.

Cornelia swung by her office, but Daniel was at her desk and on her phone, deep in conversation. She continued down the hall and stepped into the Chief of Staff's secretary's office.

"Good afternoon, Ms. Day. May I help you?"

"Good afternoon, Janet." Daniel's secretary was an institution, guiding the secretarial pool like a steady helmswoman on a storm-tossed sea. An apt metaphor after staring at the nautical wall paintings in the Navy Mess over lunch. Though Janet looked more ready for a spot of tea than to sail a ship.

In addition to her computer, Janet's desk had a notepad, a framed picture of her husband and family, and a small

Christmas tree made of copper wire curled up like branches each dangling a cheerily colored ornamental ball. The day after Thanksgiving weekend, it was the first sign she'd seen of Christmas in the White House.

Cornelia handed over the President's letter, "I suppose you can make sure this goes wherever it needs to go."

Janet read it quickly, nodded once, and set it in the center of her desk. "I'll take care of it, Ms. Day."

"No reaction?" Cornelia couldn't resist asking.

"Perhaps *About damned time!* would suffice," she raised her voice for only a moment. "That is, if you're asking for my personal thoughts." Janet smiled pleasantly. "You're enough to make me rethink retiring. I like Daniel immensely, but I rather expect you will be more fun to work for. Don't fear, ma'am—"

"Cornelia."

"Yes, ma'am. I'll stick around at least through the transition. Let's go look at your new office." She rose from her desk. Janet was trim, neatly gray-haired, and dressed in better than average Nordstrom. A single strand of pearls and matching earrings spoke of a woman from some era prior to the one she actually lived in.

Cornelia stepped over the threshold casually this time—concentrating so that Janet would have no cause to tease her —and came to a stop in the middle of the room as naturally as possible.

To her right was a grand fireplace. The Chief of Staff, *she!*, had one of the two corner offices on the same floor as the Oval Office—National Security Advisor Sienna Arnson had the other—which gave her two walls of windows. The last wall had large panoramic photos that she assumed were the Darlington's Tennessee farm.

For herself...perhaps she would see if the White House

collection or the National Archives had any renderings of the Lincoln-Douglas debates. She had studied those debates very carefully and it had become the key structure for her own successes. The most prized volume in her library was the first edition of Lincoln's collection of those debates that Mom had given her as a college graduation present.

The office's general motif was cream and white. A couch and a couple of armchairs formed a group by the fireplace. A long whitewashed-oak conference table dominated the corner window space. The open curtains gave her a view of her old office in the EEOB and to the south: the pergola and masking trees of the Oval Office patio, as well as the back of the pool's cabana. She'd never sat out on the stone-flagged patio and now she had her own private door to it.

The last corner of her office was filled with a large, wrap-around desk with several guest chairs...and a pile of folders so deep that there was little chance of seeing any guests from the big desk chair beyond.

"I swear that man does his filing by tornado," Janet huffed out. "I've never seen him hesitate to find a file, but the Lord alone knows how it's done."

Cornelia circled around enough to see that there were more piles on the floor under the desk. She didn't want to disparage her predecessor, especially as he was going to be her Vice President, but this would never do.

"I think you need a garbage can," Janet voiced the thought for her.

"Several."

"I'll call for a stack of burn bags," Janet agreed heartily. "The jumbo size."

If only it could be so simple. What she really needed was a librarian. But she wasn't about to call the one who...she looked down at the wall-to-wall carpet in some surprise.

"What is it, dear?"

Her office was exactly on top of the Situation Room. Damien's watch desk would be directly under the patio outside her window—perhaps she wouldn't be going out there. She took a deep breath and waved Janet over.

She sat in the chair Cornelia indicated.

"Okay. Let's sort through this and see what we have."

Cornelia might need a librarian, but she definitely wasn't calling Damien.

3

———

DAMIEN GLARED AT HIS PHONE.

It had rung a hundred times over the last week, but not once had it been a call to warn him that the Chief of Staff was on her way down to the Sit Room. She'd been here any number of times, slipping along in the wake of the President or the President-elect each time, and then hurrying out as if avoiding him.

Had he been too pushy? He knew he was bad about that. Every time he met an attractive woman, his mind immediately painted all of the possible scenarios. And with Cornelia Day his imagination had been working overtime. He could see her grinning easily whenever he dug deep enough to find that funny bone she struggled so hard to keep hidden—though he had yet to tip her over into laughter. He could picture quiet dinners together. And, just as easily as he could imagine how she might look morning-tousled, he could picture her growing old and how stunning an—

"Shit!"

"What's wrong?" both Bettani and Gerardo startled from

their duty watch officer positions to either side of his central seat.

"Nothing!" He was simply being his normal idiot self.

"I know that look," Bettani accused him.

"No, you don't!" He glared at her. The three of them sat on the upper tier of workstations, each with triple computer screens. Marko, the communications specialist, and Felice, the intelligence analyst, sat in the row directly in front of them, just low enough to not block anyone's sightlines to the big screens on the walls.

Marko and Felice were now turning around to look up at him.

"I absolutely know that look," Marko crowed.

"Shit!" No way this was going to get any better. Pulling on his *Marine Corps* wasn't going to save him any grief either.

"Who is she?" His coworkers exchanged looks, but no one had caught on. That was some relief.

"No way!" He informed them. A warble tone and he dove for the phone. *Saved by the bell.* He spotted the display the moment before he spoke. "Good morning, Ms. Day. How may I be of assistance?"

He could see Bettani exchanging a startled glance with Marko. They mouthed whispers at each other.

"Day?"

"The new Chief of Staff."

Their stereo *Ohs* and knowing nods had him turning away to glare at Gerardo who had the decency to find sudden interest in the data on his screens.

"Do you ever make house calls?" Cornelia's voice didn't have the businesslike brusqueness that he'd overheard during meetings in the Sit Room. Instead it was...gentler. Still business, but less fiercely so.

Then her question registered and that stopped Damien for a second. "House calls?"

"I have—"

Bettani made a small whoop of delight close behind him that stopped Cornelia cold.

"I have," she had to clear her throat to start again, "some issues here and, frankly, would appreciate the assistance of a trained librarian."

He glanced at the queue on his screen—seriously ugly at the moment. White House Chief of Staff Cornelia Day had not been neglecting her massive duties to the new administration, despite being immersed in the old one, and had inundated his team with background checks and information requests. Then Damien turned further and caught sight of Bettani's knowing smirk. That's when he decided that she could damn well double up on her workload for a while.

"I'll be there in a minute," he hung up. Anger wasn't in his usual repertoire, but he could feel it coursing through him. It built as he rose, straightened his tie, and donned his jacket.

"Gotta be all purty for your date," Bettani drew out the words in an obnoxious singsong.

He slammed his palm on the back of her chair forcing her to turn and fully face him.

Damien got right up in her face.

"You do *not*, I repeat, not *ever* talk about the White House Chief of Staff or any other senior staff with anything but the utmost respect. Not in my Sit Room. We clear?"

Bettani was wide-eyed in shock. He could see Marko's surprise out of the corner of his eye.

He slammed her chair back to facing her console, "Now

get some goddamn work done. I want that queue caught up before I return."

Damien stormed out of the room. It had never been so silent.

———

"PERHAPS THIS WASN'T A GOOD TIME," SHE GREETED HIM AS Damien arrived in her office. Cornelia could almost see curls of steam coming off his collar.

"No, it's fine," he paced from the holly-bedecked fireplace mantel to the twinkle-light framed windows and back.

She and Janet had selected carefully from the decorator's offerings and she thought that their choices had made the office cheery yet tasteful. Wishing to be somewhat non-denominational, she had vetoed the crèche for the center of her conference table in favor of a Victorian porcelain Santa's sleigh with reindeer. The effect was warm and pleasant, but Damien didn't appear to notice as he steamrollered up and down her carpet.

Perhaps, being Jewish, he didn't like any symbols of Christmas. That would make December at the White House quite annoying if he was so intolerant.

Finally he plummeted into the chair across her now immaculate desk—which bore only her portfolio and a small wire-form tree to match Janet's—practically snarling as he did so.

She merely raised an eyebrow and waited him out.

"I just made a complete jackass of myself," he sighed and continued to study something in the vicinity of his feet. "Not unusual, but I really did it spectacularly this time."

"About what?"

His eyes flickered to hers for a moment, then back to his feet.

"Okay," Cornelia did what she could to catch her breath. She wished she'd left a few of Daniel's files on her desk so that she had something to occupy her hands for a moment. She could think of several possible scenarios. First woman in the job. Or merely the first person to follow in Daniel's immensely popular footsteps. Or was it...personal?

"Let's just say," his smile grew and shifted wryly sideways as if he was finally starting to see some humor in the situation, "that I became a little defensive."

"I wouldn't know anything about that."

He laughed aloud; she'd never met someone who laughed so easily. "Do tell."

"During my first trip to the Hill as Chief of Staff, I met a wide range of aides and congressman who did not consider me to be worthy of my predecessor."

"To hell with them."

"That is not really an option. I have to—"

"No! Seriously, Ms. Day, to hell with them. If they want access to the President, this one or the next, they're going to have to go through you. They damn well better get used to it."

She'd never thought of it that way. "For Zachary Thomas as first Governor then Vice President, my responsibilities were...defensive."

"Guarding the gates like a good Marine," he nodded a solid confirmation.

"Now, it is less clear. I am discovering that I am an extension of the President's voice, or I'm trying to be."

"Do. Or do not. There is no try."

"And now you're quoting Yoda at me?"

Damien shrugged and slipped a little lower in his chair.

"Are you sure you're a Marine?"

"You asked for a librarian's help, so that's who I brought. I left the Marine downstairs," then he grimaced. "Oh brother did I."

Cornelia almost asked for details, then thought better of it. Straightening her jacket, she turned to the matters at hand.

———

DAMIEN LOVED THE GESTURE. IT WAS LIKE CAPTAIN PICARD straightening his uniform before he gave an order. Cornelia Day in command of a starship wearing a form-clinging Star Trek outfit. *Wow!* Way better than Janeway. Even better than Dr. Beverly Crusher who he'd had a weak spot for from the very first episode.

"The quantity of information flowing toward the President," Cornelia folded her hands neatly on her desk as she spoke, "is staggering. At the moment I'm trying to manage two administrations and it is completely overwhelming."

"Despite the evidence of your immaculate desk."

"Twelve burn bags for paper copies of reports I can access on the server and three new filing cabinets for the reports and memos I can't."

He could easily believe it; he'd seen Daniel's desk before.

"I'm seeking suggestions on the proper filtering and organization of information."

Now *that* was his kind of problem.

As they discussed the options he couldn't help watching her stillness. It was strictly external—her mind was moving at an incredibly rapid pace. It was as if her thought processes consumed all of her attention until there was nothing left over for her physicality. Even her eyeblinks were alarmingly wide-spaced; he could feel his own eyes going dry from unconsciously matching her steady gaze.

"One page," he finally suggested. They'd discussed a dozen different techniques: priority tagging, electronic queuing, and others.

"One page?" She tilted her head to the side, the tips of her hair now draping across her shoulder rather than brushing her collarbone. Her long neck elegantly on display. She made him want to see things that he definitely shouldn't be thinking about the Chief of Staff...though he had to admit that he had been thinking them all week.

"Mom had a colonel who used to say that if someone couldn't distill their idea down into a single page, then they hadn't finished thinking it through enough. I've never forgotten that. What's the average length of a memo delivered to your desk?"

For the first time since he'd first seen her, she opened her tablet computer. She tapped a few keys, stroked her finger down a spreadsheet column, and studied the result.

No guesses for Cornelia Day and an indexing system that included number of pages. This woman was making his inner librarian swoon with delight.

"Average is eleven pages with a first standard deviation of only three."

"Don't these people know how to communicate a thought?"

"Oddly," more taps on the screen, "other than the head speechwriter, not a one. His average memos are typically two pages and his speeches trend six minutes shorter than any prior writer's."

"Hire that man!"

"I already did," she didn't even look up from her screen.

"His assistant averages fourteen pages and eleven minutes longer than the last decade's average."

"Fire his ass!" Damien felt like he was becoming a swashbuckling captain on an old cutter. "Keelhaul the blaggard!"

Cornelia raised a single eyebrow at him, à la Mr. Spock.

"Seriously. A speechwriter who—" And then Damien snapped his mouth shut. He was talking to the White House Chief of Staff about one of her key staff members, one who'd been with the administration for over three years. That was seven kinds of inappropriate. "Sorry."

"Interesting," Cornelia mulled the thought.

"Are you channeling Mr. Spock intentionally?"

"Who? Oh, the Star Wars character? No."

Damien groaned and slapped his hands over his heart.

"What?"

"Star Trek! Not Star Wars!"

Her thin smile was unreadable. Tolerant perhaps? It goaded him on.

"You were doing great as my fantasy woman right up until that moment." Then he heard his own words and bolted upright in his chair. Unable to contain his embarrassment, he jolted to his feet. "I'm sorry, ma'am. I have deeply overstepped the bounds of propriety. Please allow me to formally apologize. If you wish to file a complaint, I will make no argument." He held parade rest, looking straight ahead at the wall.

Cornelia was a long time answering. "I've never been anyone's fantasy woman before."

"Then, if you don't mind my saying so, ma'am, every man you've met is an idiot." He sighed. "Definitely including this one."

"Sit down please, Mr. Feinman."

After checking to see that she actually meant it, he settled slowly back into the chair.

"First, let us dispose of the question regarding the assistant speechwriter."

That snapped his attention back to her, but he didn't trust himself to speak. He'd just embarrassed himself in front of his team and now in front of her and she was pretending as if nothing happened.

"I suspect," she still studied her tablet, "that the head speechwriter doesn't approve of him much. I observe here that his speeches are relegated to the less critical staff and occasions."

———

AND I OBSERVE OVER THERE A HANDSOME MAN WHO HAS JUST called me his fantasy woman.

No one had ever called her that. Her lack of allure was something she'd come to accept about herself. Her skills were in the workplace, not the bedroom.

Her lovers never remained for long. They arrived as often as she let them, but they consistently departed fast enough that there was no question who was the problem in the relationship—six-week average with a two-week first standard deviation. The outlier data points were a one-night mistake and a four-month anomaly that never should have occurred. She'd have cast out the latter except she hadn't had that many relationships and without him her averages slid downward badly.

By staying focused on the White House speechwriters, she managed to control her reactions. Not only did the compliment move her, but also Damien's instant and complete retraction. No, not retraction. He hadn't unsaid his words, he'd merely apologized for them in a remarkably sincere way.

She really didn't have time for *charming* at this moment in her life, but Damien Feinman absolutely was.

"Perhaps," he tested her silence—which was a blessing as she had no idea what to say. "Perhaps you should find a better speechwriter."

"Perhaps…" With the thought planted, it only took her a moment to recall a couple of speeches she had heard that indicated a great writer behind them. It only took her a few moments to think of who. When she did, it made her sigh.

"What's wrong?"

"He's a writer for the other party."

"So? Does he want to be writing for the President of the United States? That's the real question."

"I'll have to ask. Thank you, Damien." It was a very good idea. And it was out of the box of too-easily accepted partisanship. She'd definitely have to remember that. *Get out of the box.*

"My pleasure, ma'am." So, he was going to remain safe behind his formality. It wasn't mere politeness. She could hear the Marine ingrained deep in him by both the Corps and his mother.

"Stepping back to the one-page concept," she wasn't yet ready to confront the main topic that still lay untouched upon her desk.

"Yes," Damien cleared his throat and relaxed slightly. "The entire idea must be presentable in a single sheet. There can be and typically should be supporting documentation, but the core of it must be pared down to the essentials. Two pages at the very most, but push for one."

"Perhaps I should require it to be double-spaced as well."

Damien's burst of laughter had her looking up from the tablet, which had long since blanked to save its battery.

She raised the Spock eyebrow at him again. Did Damien actually believe that she didn't know about Spock? She'd had a crush on the half-Vulcan ever since her mom had introduced her to the classic Trek as a pre-teen. She'd felt like a traitor switching her allegiance from Nimoy to Quinto as an adult, but at least he was within a decade of her own age. Teasing a man was not in her standard repertoire, but Damien was so sure of himself that she was discovering the opportunity difficult to resist.

"I like the evil way that you think," Damien was slowly relaxing back into his chair. "I'd give them the single-spaced permission, but you'd best specify a minimum font size or you'll go blind in short order."

"Definitely," she agreed. It was easy to share his smile on that. "As to the final point..."

Cornelia took a deep breath. She couldn't think of the right way to confront it. The early December darkness had fallen even before they'd started and now it was well past time to leave. Janet had signaled from the door an hour ago that the President had returned to the Residence for the night and she was going home.

For her entire first week as the Chief of Staff she'd been avoiding Damien because...

Because she was attracted to him? He was a very attractive man, she'd have to be dead to not notice. And she wasn't.

Perhaps she should go out of the box, the one she kept drawn so carefully about herself. She took a deep breath and decided to be brave.

"Damien. Do you have any plans for dinner?"

His face displayed a brief battle between surprise and delight.

When the latter won, she decided that perhaps she didn't mind being someone's fantasy woman. For as long as it lasted anyway.

4

———

DAMIEN HAD TO STRUGGLE AGAINST BEING DAZZLED.

"Take me to your favorite place to eat."

Had she said *restaurant* he'd have struggled to think of somewhere nice, but *to eat* had only one answer.

"It isn't upscale or Californian or—"

"That's fine."

So, he'd taken her at her word.

Ten minutes on the Metro and a couple minutes of chilly walking at either end didn't seem to affect her in the slightest. Donning only a stylish but understated burgundy wool coat and thin black gloves, she appeared untouched by the freezing evening. Her scarf was a cheery knit in Christmas reds and greens; it gave her color and made her eyes and chill-reddened cheeks appear brighter.

He second-guessed himself all of the way to Molly Malone's. The big oak tree out front had long since lost its leaves for the year, but it was so thickly strung with multi-colored Christmas lights that there seemed to be as many bulbs as there had been leaves. It lit the whole stretch of sidewalk as if the tree were the shining Star of Bethlehem.

The moment Cornelia stepped through the door, she shouted over the general roar of noise, "It's perfect!"

"Glad you approve!" A gorgeous, urbanite, DC insider who thought a cozy pub was perfect place for dinner. What wasn't to like.

Molly's was the best Irish pub outside of Ireland. The brick walls dated back nearly as far as the Marine Barracks across the street—the oldest in the country. *Irish* decorated the walls—there was no other good word for it. Old cruise line posters, paintings of ships, photos of rambling greensward and rocky coasts, all capped by a massive picture of the mythical warrior-hero Finn MacCool. All of the trimwork was in rich woods that really did hearken back to the mother land—even for a fourth-generation Brooklynite like himself.

For the season, tiny live Christmas trees in pots had appeared on every available ledge and surface. Wreaths adorned the few open spaces on the brick walls, and painfully bright stars shaped from white neon lights only enhanced the normally gaudy atmosphere of the place.

However, he'd forgotten it was Friday night. The downstairs booths and bar were packed solid and the wall of conversation was nearly as impenetrable.

"You brought me to a Marine bar?" Cornelia leaned in close enough for him to hear her, smell her, practically feel the heat from her body despite her coat.

"I did." He had. And once again he was second-guessing himself. The place was filled with them. "The Marine Barracks is directly across the street. Sorry, I wasn't thinking."

"You dare to bring a woman to a bar filled with Marines at their prime? You really are a brave man. Do you think I can find a handsome flute player to take me home?"

"I'll snap his damned pipe if he tries," Damien growled out, earning him a smile and a gloved hand tucked about his elbow. Of course she'd know that the Marine Band was housed at the oldest Marine barracks in the country. The location selected by Thomas Jefferson himself when they were laying out the city.

"Let's try upstairs."

And then he laughed aloud.

She looked at him quizzically but he just shook his head.

She had elicited exactly the response from him that she'd intended—a Marine-like snap and growl. The thing she probably didn't understand, was that he meant it. *Really* meant it. He wasn't merely feeling protective about Cornelia; he was feeling possessive.

It wasn't his place, but if another man tried to touch her, he'd have to be careful not to punch him. And wasn't that the biggest joke of all. *Damien Feinman, gone on a woman.*

A table vacated just as they finished battling their way up the big staircase to the second floor. A quick dive and grab and they got it before anyone else.

He was about to take her coat when a slap on his back knocked him into her. Only a quick hand against the brick wall and another around her waist kept them from both going to the floor.

"Look who crawled out from under his big white rock!" Mick was waving over a group of Marine Intelligence guys who must have arrived close behind them.

"What the hell are you doing here?" Damien tried to snarl it out but he was too busy focusing on letting go of Cornelia. His hand didn't want to leave her waist. She might be impossibly lean, but he felt her strength as well. And so warm though her thin silk blouse. His hand had slipped inside both her coat and her unfastened designer jacket when he'd grabbed her.

"Training a bunch of plebes. Intel 101—Marine style—for Career Day. *Here's what we do. Come join us!* Same old, same old. You know the drill."

He did; it had worked well enough on him—eighteen and trying to figure out how to afford University of North Carolina at Chapel Hill's stellar library program. Naval ROTC had paved the way. Doubling down on political science had been his golden ticket.

In moments his quiet dinner with Cornelia Day had turned into a free-for-all with the two of them trapped against the back wall as more and more people showed up. Soon there were seven of them at a table for four.

"Christ, Lady," Brion looked at Cornelia. "What the hell is a looker like you doing with a loser like Damien? Please tell me you have more of a sense of humor than his usual pickups."

Before Damien could leap to her defense, Cornelia planted an elbow on the table and her chin on her palm. He didn't even know her spine unbent enough to be able to do that. It did leave him sitting a little behind her and able to follow her shoulders' lines. Very nice indeed.

"Maybe I should take the Fifth on that until I know more," she faced them as smoothly as she did everything. "His usual lot?"

"Analysts," Vaccaro joined in. "He's got this wicked weak spot for hard-core data analysts. Some are cute enough, but frankly boring as hell."

"Tell us you're not boring as hell."

"Yeah. Or we'll have to go find another table."

Please! Damien thought loudly but was unable to get a

word in edgewise around his friends. He checked on Cornelia, but she was giving no sign that any of this was bothering her.

"Naw, mate," Caron leaned in. "Not an open table in the lot. 'Sides, you see any others as fine-looking as her to spend an evening with? No offense, ma'am. But you are a real pleasure to be sitting near."

"You sure you're with him?" Mick tipped his head toward Damien in disgust. "Any of us would be glad to show you what a real Marine is like."

"A real Marine?"

She was answered by a chorus of, "Aye!" and "You betcha!"

"I don't think so," she sat up once again, ever so primly perfect. "I didn't hear a single 'oorah' in the bunch. So apparently, not a Marine in sight. What is a damsel to do?"

The guys all looked properly chagrined.

Damien burst out laughing and before he could stop himself, gave her a brief hug around the shoulders. She was amazing. And felt amazing.

"You're incredible," he whispered in the moment that she let herself tip into him.

"Didn't get an oorah from you either," she whispered back.

"Librarian first. Marine second. But I'll oorah for you anytime you want."

"So do it."

"Oorah!" He managed a good one before the laughter overtook him. It was echoed up and down the restaurant by any number of patrons. The call echoed from downstairs as well.

More importantly, she leaned into him a moment longer,

before sitting upright once more. No woman, dressed or not, had ever felt so good in his arms.

"That sounds like my call!" A deep voice spoke from the head of the table.

Damien looked up then scrambled to his feet as did the other Marines. They all snapped sharp salutes even though none of them were in uniform. General Arnson returned it smartly.

"Crap! When a bunch of intel geeks salute me like it means something, makes me wonder if I'm getting old."

Vaccaro found the general a chair and they all squeezed in tighter. It left Cornelia constantly bumping Damien from shoulder to hip. The turn of the corner on the other side kept her from nudging up against Brion.

"Ms. Day," the general nodded. "Been hearing good things about you from my daughter."

"Your daughter?"

————

"Sienna," Damien prompted her.

She inspected the newcomer. If his daughter was National Security Advisor Sienna Arnson, that meant this distinguished gentleman was Brigadier General Edward Arnson. He headed up HMX-1, the helicopter squadron responsible for Marine One and the thirty other VIP transport and support rotorcraft. His reputation was beyond sterling.

"A pleasure to meet you, sir. I've traveled aboard your aircraft with the Vice President."

She managed to keep her smile to herself as all of the others around the table looked at her in surprise.

"And you call yourselves Marine Intelligence," the general sounded disgusted but his eyes gave away his amusement. "Not a one of you dolts thought to ask her name?"

"They didn't," she couldn't resist rubbing it in. "Apparently I am merely 'a looker' who was picked up by a passing Marine because she couldn't help herself around him." She did her best to bat her eyelashes at Damien and had never felt so ridiculous.

He, however, looked very pleased with himself at the moment.

She rather liked that the others had sought him out and were willing to tease her. It said a great deal about Damien and the closeness he engendered in his friends. A skill she knew that she lacked but could definitely admire.

And teasing was not something she was used to. She'd taken the palm-on-chin pose from some movie, she couldn't remember which one but it had been accepted. That she'd been able to give back as good as she got rather surprised her.

Damien slid an arm across the back of her chair as if staking his territory. Cornelia would have to see about him not getting too self-assured. She considered a gentle elbow in the ribs, but couldn't think how to make it look normal rather than something from a self-defense class.

The general shook his head sadly at the state of affairs, doing only a moderate job of hiding his own smile.

"Day," Brion twisted to her in surprise. "Cornelia Day? The new White House Chief of Staff?"

"A glimmer of light at last," the general groaned.

"Holy hell, mate," Caron smacked Damien hard on the arm. "Good on ya!"

"You see, Ms. Day?" The general looked at her, a friendly

smile lighting his face. "This is what they give me to work with. I wish you better luck with that one." The gnarled finger that he pointed at Damien wasn't threatening. Instead it was as if he was pointing out the best of poor choices.

She looked around the table and decided that if these were the *poor choices* then the Marine Corps was in impressively good shape.

"I need a beer," the general groaned even more dramatically.

"Make it two and I'll join you," Cornelia replied with some bit of humor she hadn't known she possessed.

"That's a deal, Ms. Day. We'll leave the rest of this lot to fend for themselves."

———

THE MEAL HAD PASSED IN A SINGLE BREATH.

Damien had breathed in a quick gasp anticipating total disaster when the others joined them, and breathed out several hours, a good meal, and a couple of pitchers later.

The general unwound enough, something Damien hadn't seen in a decade of knowing him, to tell war stories. From being an eighteen-year-old hothead helo pilot in the last days of the Vietnam War, up to his nephew and niece-in-law flying for the Night Stalkers—the famed Henderson and Beale.

They'd discussed the latest non-classified intel over Guinness stew and Irish bangers. Russia being ever more rabid. The disasters of Southwest Asia overshadowing the disasters of the Middle East.

As the meal progressed he could see more and more how his peers took to testing their ideas on Cornelia. She might not be a trained intel officer, but her insightful questions even had the general harrumphing a few times.

Damien himself wasn't surprised at all, yet more than once she forced his thinking down another layer with her questions.

Her questions.

"Do you have opinions of your own?" Damien wasn't sure quite where that came from.

"Excuse me?" She sounded affronted. Some of the others looked askance at him as well.

"What I mean is, your questions are fantastic. You really make us think about our assumptions. But I'm not sure what Cornelia Day is thinking."

"It's not my place."

"Not your place?" Caron nearly exploded. "Lady, if it's not yours, then whose is it?"

"The President and the Vice President. Policy is not part of my job. My duties are to promote the success of the President's agenda. No more. No less."

That earned her silent consideration from around the table.

"So, no thinking for yourself?" Mick teased.

Damien had slowly learned to read Cornelia's body language. Even partway into her second beer, she still sat like a dancer. Her sense of humor remained as it had started, smart and sharp when she was applying it and nonexistent when she was thinking on other matters. His question and the table's follow-up stiffened her already straight spine.

"My thoughts?"

Uh-oh.

Mick nodded amiably, unaware of the juggernaut that was about to land on his head.

Damien checked and noticed that she had the general's full attention. So he too had learned to read her. Or perhaps, because of his daughter being the National Security Advisor, he understood the true caliber implied by Cornelia being a senior-level White House staffer.

"My thought is that you Marine intel boys need to get your heads out of your asses."

The shock of silence rippled around the table.

Damien kept his smile to himself. *This* was the Cornelia Day that he'd seen in his files. He'd begun to doubt her existence, having only conversed with the thoughtful, even-tempered woman prior to this moment.

"Your mandate is to gather and present the information needed by your forward forces. There are a hundred and eighty-two thousand active-duty personnel who depend on your information. They are in need of *tactical* intel. Everything I've heard tonight has been *strategic* in nature—not even that. It has been top-tier political in consideration and as I'm sure Damien can tell you, not the most accurate or well thought out because you are basing your assumptions on tactical data. If you wish to work for the Defense Intelligence Agency, the NSA, and the half dozen others who operate at the strategic level, then go there and do that."

Nobody at the table appeared to be breathing.

"You are Marine officers. Those data analysts you look down on are dealing in facts, not projection modeling and definitely not conjecture. At your level of operation, your duty is to the men and women out there on the front lines. I hope that what you've been saying tonight wasn't the speech you gave to the plebes earlier today. If you're wondering why Damien is working at the White House and not you, it's because he embodies these distinctions in his thoughts and in the service he provides."

A few of the guys actually blushed as they looked to him for his response. General Arnson was keeping his thoughts to himself.

"Cornelia," Damien spoke to get her attention, to haul her back from the sharp cliff edge she had walked out onto. "I need you"—to take a breath—"to come teach at my next class at NIU. The students at the National Intelligence University really need to hear that distinction from someone more convincing than me."

She nodded once sharply, whether acknowledging the end of her rant, or his invitation to NIU was accepted was unclear.

"My pleasure."

———

"I don't know what came over me," Cornelia hugged her coat more tightly around her. It was no colder outside, but she suddenly felt chilled to the bone.

"Whatever it was, it was utterly magnificent," Damien was practically chortling as he squeezed his left hand over where hers was tucked around his right elbow.

"But I ruined the dinner," she'd been working it so carefully. Had begun to feel that these men might actually like her for being, well, not the woman who had told them they were full of it in front of a one-star general. God she was hopeless.

"Not for a second," Damien practically crowed with delight.

"It's fine for you to be happy. You didn't just alienate an entire department of the military."

A light snow began falling, fluttering and glittering past the streetlights. She normally loved this moment when the city turned magical. Colorado had thickened her California blood but she had never gotten over the wonder of her first major snowfall after joining the Governor's office. But it was hard to enjoy it when she was busy blowing up her career. And after only one week on the job!

"I now represent the President of the United States. I should never have spoken—"

"The truth?" Damien's voice turned unexpectedly harsh. "They were all trying to impress you. That's a male intel officer's form of flirting: *Look at how smart I am.* Well, you called their bluff. Gave the general some food for thought as well."

"I couldn't even look at him," Cornelia wanted to hide her face against Damien's shoulder.

"Well, you impressed the hell out of the only two people at the table that mattered."

"Who was the other one..." she trailed off when Damien glanced at her sidelong. "I—"

She would keep her questions and opinions to herself from now on.

The snow was staying light and calming. Apparently they were walking back to the White House. It was an hour away at a brisk clip, the only speed appropriate for this weather, and she didn't mind even though she wasn't properly dressed for it. She needed to burn off some of the nervous energy coursing through her.

The rest of Barracks Row was fully decked out for Christmas: frame shop photos of Santa Class, bicycles with red and green flashing lights, a kitchen store window filled with holiday cookie cutters. It was a three-block long line of Christmas cheer and twinkle lights and she couldn't wait to get out of it. She finally felt as if she could breathe when they reached the end of the Row and turned left onto Pennsylvania Avenue.

"What were you going to say?" Damien prompted her when she slowed from mad dash to merely panicked hurry.

"I was going to ask something rude."

"Don't stop now, Cornelia. You're on a roll."

"I—" but she couldn't go any further.

"You're going to ask why I'm the other one who mattered?" He asked it with a level of perception and a degree of frankness she was truly coming to appreciate in him.

She nodded and held onto his arm so that he wouldn't walk away in fury.

"It's not the same reason as the general."

Cornelia tried to puzzle it out. Damien could slow down her intel requests, but she expected that he had too much integrity for that. He could bad mouth her to other Sit Room staff causing the next two years to become decidedly awkward in the Situation Room...as if she wasn't doing enough of that job herself.

He still didn't answer as they walked past the bright Capitol Dome, then the towering blue pinnacle of the Capitol Christmas Tree out front, before they began walking the length of the National Mall. Through the glassed-front of the Air and Space Museum she could see the great planes and spaceships of the last century. And some century yet to come—the original shooting model of the Starship *Enterprise* had been placed in the same hall as the Apollo LEM and Chuck Yeager's X-1 that had broken the sound barrier.

Face it. Head-on. Deep breath. Doesn't help. "Why then are you the other one who matters?"

"Explanation or demonstration?" Damien finally asked in a voice so soft she barely heard it.

"Demonstration?" What did he mean by that? She meant it as a question, he took it as her choice.

Using her left hand as guidance where it still tucked about his elbow, he turned her into his arms. One moment they were walking side-by-side beneath the snow-spattered sky. The next she was being kissed in front of the glass wall of the museum.

This was definitely a Marine-first-librarian-second kiss. She assumed that he'd let her loose...if she wanted an out. But from the first instant, the cold of the winter's night was scorched from her body. Her pulse roared to life.

Had she known that she wanted to kiss him?

Perhaps.

Had she seriously considered it?

That answer blurred as she sank into it. Neither of them were demonstrating much beyond their most primal, animal intelligence. She wrapped her arms around the bulk of his Navy pea coat and held him tightly so that he wouldn't think to stop.

Wouldn't think.

Don't think.

She sagged against him, trusting the Marine to hold her upright because her own legs weren't up to it.

Courtesy of their thick coats and his lovely build, her arms could barely reach around his chest and shoulders to clasp behind him. Yet his strong arms overlapped as they wrapped about her and held on.

He offered to pull back, to make this kiss as merely a moment of heat.

Cornelia wasn't ready to let go and kept him pulled in tight against her.

Some passing motorist beeped their car horn in a cheery pattern.

Only when her heart raced so fast that she couldn't catch her breath did she break the kiss. She leaned her head against his shoulder, not yet ready to let go.

"Holy hell, Cornelia. What was that about?"

"Stop being an analyst for a moment, please." She could feel his chuckle better than she could hear it despite their thick coats separating them.

"Well, if that's your standard kiss—"

It wasn't.

"—I can't wait to see what comes next."

"Analyst."

He shrugged at her accusation.

Her pulse and breathing finally slowed enough for her to be aware once more that she had legs and by some miracle they were still able to support her.

"That," she managed to stand upright and pat a hand on Damien's cheek, "wasn't my standard *anything*."

"Well, it certainly worked for me, ma'am, whatever it was."

It had worked for her as well.

"You okay to keep walking?"

Not trusting herself to speak, she nodded.

"Good, because I'm not. Okay if I lean on you?"

Slowly he tucked her hand once more about his elbow and headed along the sidewalk once more. Except—

"That's the Capitol Dome," Damien stated with some surprise.

"It is," Cornelia sought her best disenchanted tourist voice. "And that is its Christmas tree on the front lawn."

"We've already been by here."

"We have," she managed to keep the surprise out of her voice.

With a ceremonial nod that might have been part bow, he turned them about and once more they were headed back toward the White House.

Cornelia never thought a giggle was a seemly utterance for a woman grown. So she fought down the desire to do so and simply said, "Thank you, kind sir."

"Kind sir, my ass. Kind sirs don't wonder how many minutes it is until we can try that without our winter coats."

"Many."

"Crap!"

"I could invite you up for a nightcap, but I live another fifteen minute walk west of the White House," Cornelia tried to parse the words as they slipped out of her mouth. If she understood them as individual words, she might be able to edit, correct, and verify prior to release. But they slipped out as a single cogent thought far beyond her control.

Damien guided them past the gauntlet of national museums and most of the way to the Washington Monument before he spoke again.

"Are you sure?"

"I'm not sure of anything." However, "Except that the answer to that is yes." Cornelia didn't try to analyze her response. For once in her life she would live in the moment. For this one time she'd let go and do something not because it was right, but because she wanted to.

They walked past the National Christmas Tree on the Ellipse, fully decorated, but still dark for tomorrow's tree-lighting ceremony. The silence wrapped warm about them in the frosty air.

———

Getting to Cornelia's condo was either the longest or the shortest walk of his life. It would have seemed impossible that she'd invited him back to her place, if not for that kiss. Damien had expected her kiss to be as smooth and perfect as she was. Instead, there'd been a mind-blanking heat that had fired up his body on a cold winter's night. He couldn't try that again soon enough—he had to know if it had been real.

And yet, walking down the length of The Mall through the falling snow, passing monument after monument with her hand once again on his arm—like a couple who'd been together forever—had passed far too quickly. Again the idiot-around-women part of his brain was imagining what it would be like to make this walk together each night, each month, each—

Typical! He really needed to get control of his thoughts. *Not a chance of that with Cornelia beside him.*

They walked in silence through the snow. When she turned off the sidewalk in front of a beautiful old brickwork building renovated into condos, she stopped.

He didn't ask again if she was sure. He didn't want to break the peace that stood between them.

Instead he simply waited.

She didn't turn to study his face. Nor did she drag him ahead like some overeager wanton. Cornelia simply kept her hand on his arm and, after only the briefest hesitation, continued up the front walkway as if they'd done it a thousand times.

"Ms. Day. Sir," the elderly doorman welcomed them after buzzing them through the secure door.

"Thank you, Mr. Rivers."

He handed Cornelia her mail and they rode the elevator to the third floor.

Her condo was as neat as her office. A small, but cozy one bedroom with a kitchen that looked little used. Soft, indirect lighting. A full-wall bookcase that was filled with both political memoir and thriller. There was little art on the walls other than a few pictures of her with the President-elect before he was the President-elect. They spanned over a decade of time, but she looked little changed. All of the way back to the high school graduation photo standing beside her mother, she looked like a grown woman.

The silence echoed in his ears as she hung up her coat then his in the closet.

He waited. He didn't want a nightcap. He didn't want coffee and a bit of phony chit-chat on the tastefully pale-green sofa. Her apartment, like her clothing, was a palate of neutrals or pastel shades. No strong statements here— except the woman herself, placing her shoes in the bottom of the hall closet.

Her presence shouted in the neutral room as loudly as a vermillion wall hanging or blaring music.

"God, Cornelia. You're so—" stepping close she rested a warm finger on his lips.

"I've never understood games or small talk," she whispered from mere inches away. And she replaced her finger with a brush of her lips.

"And I've never met a woman who was so forthright."

"You fascinated me from the first moment, Damien."

"Fascinated? Are you sure you aren't channeling Spock?"

"Who?" But this time her smile spoke volumes to him. And he realized that it should have the first time as well.

"Crap!" Damien growled. "And I totally fell for it that you somehow had missed a whole segment of American culture."

She ran a hand up over his chest, looking down at her

fingers as she did so. He was left to look at the top of her head as she traced a line of fire upward.

"Let me guess. You're one of those girls, women, who had a total crush on Spock."

"Had?" She said it so coyly that he couldn't help laughing. "And you strike me as a Beverly Crusher type."

"No," he lied. "Troi for me. In the Season One cheerleader outfit."

"Liar." Cornelia didn't make it a question. "Analysts they said at dinner."

"I'll kill them later."

"You always go for the brains." She leaned in to rub her nose on his neck. "Me too," she whispered.

"Guilty," he slid his hands onto her waist and up her ribcage.

It *was* fascinating: how she felt against the curve of his palm and fingers, how her lips tasted of no lipstick or balm, but rather just a hint of the espresso dark chocolate pie they'd shared and a slight spiciness that had nothing to do with their meals.

"Besides Crusher has a great body, just different." He was on the verge of saying "Like yours." But he didn't. Not because of tact, never one of his strengths, but because there was no way that anyone could feel as good as Cornelia.

His tie had disappeared when he wasn't paying attention. And his shirt was halfway unbuttoned.

"And if you're trying to spoil my fantasy woman image of you, being able to knowledgeably discuss Star Trek isn't helping you out at all."

"Do you always talk so much?"

Damien considered for a moment. "Usually, but I'll make an exception in your case." He shifted his hands to her breast and behind. Then he pulled her back into the hard kiss he wanted to try again.

They groaned in unison at how good it was.

Except for a brief foray to the bathroom for protection, they didn't make another sound as he melted onto the white living room carpet and pulled her down on top of him. The couch was too far away.

5

———

CORNELIA HADN'T SLEPT LIKE THAT IN A LONG TIME. FOR ONE thing, she was warm, an unusual event with only the sheet over her. Damien was delightfully warm to sleep next to. For another thing, her morning workout sessions might tone her body, but it didn't wring her out into limp-dishrag territory the way last night's activities had. A simpatico energy had run between them, draining her physically and energizing her...her what?

Her thoughts were as languid as her body at the moment; a very unusual state for her.

Her emotions...were as strange and distant as ever. Except they weren't the *same* as ever. They were—

"You're thinking awfully hard for seven in the morning," Damien's whispered greeting tickled her ear.

"I'm—Wait! Seven?" She scrabbled around for some covers, finally hauling the blanket around her as she crawled out of bed.

"Whoa!" Damien made a grab for her that she managed to dodge, but he snagged the blanket. He held one end as she held the other over her breasts and hips.

"But it's seven," the need to get moving coursed through her.

"It's Saturday."

"But it's seven." She always finished her stepper workout by six-thirty, shower and breakfast by seven, at the White House or the EEOB by seven-thirty.

"Cornelia. Take a breath. Today is Saturday," as if she was a child and hadn't heard him the first time.

"That doesn't matter. You wouldn't believe everything on my desk."

"Your desk is immaculate and empty."

She tried to give him a withering look, but Damien didn't seem to be the kind of man to wither. Simply because her queue was electronic didn't make it any smaller. Her inbox inherited from Daniel filled three file cabinets and what had appeared in the last week filled most of another—she was beginning to understand why Daniel had filed the way he did. Yesterday's discussion with Damien meant that she now had a plan of attack. A quiet Saturday, if there was such a thing in the White House, would be the perfect opportunity to start implementing it.

"Okay," he shrugged and offered one of his charming smiles as if that was going to work. "Come back to bed long enough to not have an awkward morning-after and I'll go in and be your assistant for the day."

"It isn't awkward. I simply have to get to work."

"But how do I know that you *sincerely* shared your stunning body and incredible sexual prowess with me if I don't have confirmation in the morning that it wasn't just an illusion."

"Because I actually did," like she'd never had with another. Damien had unlocked some strange key inside her that she hadn't known existed. She had wanted things, done things, like she never had before. And Damien had responded like a good Marine, taking the least little instruction and following it to the very limit.

Resisting his light tug on the other end of her blanket would have been easier without his smile. Sliding back into bed once she was awake was a sinful act.

But it was nothing compared to what happened for the next half hour.

————

DAMIEN WAS IN A DAZE THAT ALLOWED CORNELIA TO SLIP away and head to the shower. He lay still, unable to move. Unwilling to leave the sheets that carried her subtle scent. The woman made his head spin, but her body...

"I need to find a saint to pray to," because he needed this to be real.

"An odd choice for a Jewish man," Cornelia had taken the fastest shower in the world. He'd thought to join her there, but had obviously missed his few seconds of opportunity.

He turned from burying his face in her pillow to looking at her standing at the bathroom threshold and drying herself off. Her leanness wasn't model-worthy: ribs protruding and some fear that she'd fall over in a strong breeze. Instead, she was gloriously slender. Her curves weren't blatant, they wouldn't fit her so well if they were. She was a subtle woman in both thought and form. Of course what she did between the sheets, or out on the living room rug, was anything but subtle.

He smiled as she buffed one long leg and then the other with a thick towel. He had very clear memories of how she had wrapped those long limbs about him. And even clearer memories of how she'd looked as the pleasure took her. It would have been humbling that he could please her so if not for his own memories. He'd *never* had a woman like Cornelia Day. Her transformation from elegant urbanite to passionate lover made the experience only that much more incredible.

Again, between one eyeblink and the next, she had dressed and, now standing close by, looking down at him. Perhaps in celebration of the weekend, she wore designer jeans and a simple turtleneck rather than one of her moderately terrifying and utterly delectable silk-and-wool outfits. She even wore fur-trimmed, buckle boots that he'd bet were the latest style—selected with maximum efficiency, of course—and he had to admit that they looked very cute on her. He slipped a hand out from under the warm covers to slide it up the back of her leg and over her lovely behind.

For a moment she merely looked down at him.

Had he been wrong? Had last night—

Then, without a sound, her eyes slid closed for a moment and he could see the sigh that was too soft to hear.

"God, Cornelia. You—"

And with that the White House Chief of Staff was suddenly back in the room. "Stay as long as you like. Don't bother coming in. It's your day off."

"It's yours too," he called as she stepped from his caress and strode off toward the bedroom door.

She waved a hand over her head and was gone. A moment later the front door snicked shut. Then it opened, he heard a rattle in the front closet as she grabbed a coat, and then she really was gone.

He managed not to laugh aloud until she was gone again. Her being flustered enough to forget her coat was infinitely reassuring to his male ego.

Damien rolled out of bed, then made it with military corners and wondered if that would be up to her standards. She'd left him a fresh towel, a new razor about the size of his pinkie, and no coffee. When he checked the fridge after his Navy-fast shower, he saw that no breakfast—or much of anything else—was ever served from this kitchen. He made a mental note to cook for her sometime.

The doorman was a younger man than the night before. He had the discretion to make no comment as he watched Damien leave, but his look said plenty.

The morning air had a sharp bite to it. An inch of snow slickened the sidewalks and turned the city of marble even whiter than it usually was.

He could take Cornelia at her word and enjoy his weekend. Thankfully, he wasn't that much of an idiot.

Spying out the bootprints in the bright morning sunlight that must have been hers—a snow often turned DC into a city of shut-ins—he traced her path to a coffee shop. With a large drip in one hand and a breakfast burrito in the other, he strode out to make up some time as he followed her the rest of the way to the White House. *Wherever* she wanted to lead, he was more than willing to follow.

———

CORNELIA DIDN'T KNOW WHY SHE'D FELT SUCH A NEED TO GET out of the apartment and away from Damien. Whatever it was didn't nudge, it shoved. She wasn't running from a morning confrontation—she wouldn't mind more waking confrontations like that one. Her body felt glorious beyond any merely physical workout.

And, she took a deep breath as she passed through White House security at the Southwest Gate, she didn't mind if those future events were with Marine Corps Captain Damien Feinman. No one had ever made her feel even half as special as he had with the simplest gesture.

He didn't treat her like a woman—he treated her like a miracle.

Fantasy woman. Was that her problem? That he had her up on a pedestal for some incomprehensible reason? No more than she him. Intelligent, funny, handsome, and the things that he could do with his hands had made her want to scream with the intensity. She was—

A complete and utter basket case.

Entrance security cleared her into the empty West Wing Foyer. To her right would be the weekend watch officers in the Sit Room. The irony of that was only starting to grow on her. It was actually three large conference rooms, two smaller ones, and a massive central area which was occupied by the tiered desk of the watch. The ever-so-famous President's Situation Room was only one small briefing room off to the side. It was far more Damien's domain than the President's. Yet so much happened there.

She worked her way upstairs. The West Wing cleaning staff was long gone and only a few hardcores like herself were in this early on a snowy Saturday. Most of the light came from the understated Christmas décor that was typical for the West Wing. The Residence might get all dandified for the public tours, but here there was only the occasional wreath or the icicle lights dangling above the stairwell. For a change, it was peaceful.

So much had happened here in the last week. In the Sit Room on Monday she'd become White House Chief of Staff and met Damien. Now, six days later she was overwhelmed by the former, and the latter? Was overwhelming her as well.

All she needed was one quiet day to get her head wrapped around what was going on, maybe two. To catch up for one single moment so that she could—

"Oh good, you're here," President-elect Zachary came up behind her with Daniel in tow as she stepped into Janet's office. Her own desk phone was ringing.

Yes, a perfect, quiet day. Not a chance.

She waved for them to follow her through Janet's office and into her own as she rushed to catch the call.

With it being the weekend and Janet not in, someone had to really sell it to get past the White House switchboard.

She hit the speaker button then moved to hang up her coat and turn on some lights. The sun was still low to the east, leaving her office in a twilit shadow.

"We have a Mr. Pejman on the line for you. He says that you met him during the disaster in Italy. He has been calling every hour on the hour since five a.m."

She didn't recall a Mr. Pejman, but she certainly recalled the Italy disaster. A man-made avalanche had killed a number of global senior-level leaders at a climate conference. It was also where Zachary Thomas had clinched the election even before he started his campaign, by how many people he had fought to save over the next two days. She had been at his side for all of it, but she recalled no Mr. Pejman.

She glanced at the President-elect, but he shrugged his shoulders as well. Cornelia was his memory for things like names. Even through all of the people they had been in contact with during that rescue.

"Send his call through."

"Ms. Day?"

"Mr. Pejman, how can I help you?"

"Are we private, Ms. Day?"

She glanced at Daniel and Zachary in time to see Damien walk in. He opened his mouth but she put a finger over her lips to silence him. Calling every hour on the hour early on a Saturday didn't sound like a social call. She'd been Chief of Staff for less than a week and she wasn't going to tackle this one alone.

"We are private, Mr. Pejman."

Pejman? Damien mouthed to her.

She nodded.

He ducked out of the room and she could see him bending over to use Janet's computer.

"I should very much like to meet with you in person, Ms. Day."

"May I ask what this is about?"

"I am afraid that it is not a matter to be discussed in such a way." She almost had his accent. Middle-eastern? Arabic? No, Farsi. Regrettably, Persian wasn't one of her languages—she was more of a college-French- or Italian-tourist-style linguist.

"Then I fear that I can't help you with—"

Damien rushed back into the room and handed her a slip of paper.

Pejman: Asst. to UN ambassador Iran.

"It is very important that I speak with you in person, Ms. Day."

"Where are you, Mr. Pejman?"

"Katz's Deli at one o'clock."

"Katz's?"

"I will see you then, Ms. Day." And the line went dead.

"Where's Katz's?" she asked the others.

Zachary and Daniel shook their heads.

"Oh my Lord God, Defender of the Universe!" Damien

burst out. "Deliver me from this bunch of heathens. It's the best deli there is."

"I've been in DC for eight years and I haven't heard of it."

"It's in New York. Lower East Side. Absolutely awesome!"

"New York?" Cornelia shook her head. "I am *not* going to New York."

"What," Zachary pointed, "is that slip that Damien gave you?"

She handed it over.

Zachary and Daniel studied it for a long moment, exchanged one of their mind-reading glances, then turned back to her in unison. That habit was going to get very irritating as this administration progressed.

Then she read their looks. "No. I'm *not* going to New York today."

They waited.

"I'm not a field operative. I'm barely a Chief of Staff. How can I be Chief of Staffing if I'm not even here?"

"Where are you going?" The President stepped into the room. Even on a Saturday he was well dressed, with a blazer but no tie. More formal than his first administration. It was as if he was practicing for the role of elder statesman.

"Katz's Deli," Damien replied for her, clearly enjoying the game at her expense. Probably payback for her Mr. Spock tease.

"Oh," President Matthews smiled. "Get the pastrami. Though the corned beef is awfully good too. I tell you what, order both and bring me back whichever you don't want. Why are you going there?"

Zachary handed him the slip of paper. "He wants to meet with Cornelia at one p.m. today. Wouldn't say what was up over the phone. He seemed rather cagey about it."

The President's *bonhomie* evaporated. "Pejman?"

Cornelia glanced at the desk clock that she'd unearthed from beneath Daniel's stack of five consecutive monthly reports on the ice melt along the Arctic Northwest Passage —all of which had said the same thing and four of which had now been burned.

"If I have to get to New York by one, the train will take too long. I need to see if there's a shuttle flying with room on it. Even if there is I'll be late," She cursed herself for luxuriating in bed with Damien. If she'd gotten up at her normal time, she'd have been here several call attempts earlier.

"She doesn't understand how this works," the President smiled at her. "Damien, do you have the number?"

Damien walked up to her phone and offered a saucy wink as he dialed. Then he handed the handset to the President.

"Hello, this is the President for Eddie."

Cornelia wondered who in the world Eddie might be.

"Eddie? Peter Matthews here. My Chief of Staff is headed to New York. She'll be to your location in fifteen minutes. Great. Thanks," he handed her the phone and she hung it up.

Damien picked up one of the other lines at the conference table and made a quick call.

"I take it that I'm going to New York." She didn't make it a question and no one corrected her.

"Take him with you," President Matthews pointed at Damien. "If ever there was a man who won't shut up about New York pastrami, he's it. Or maybe you should leave him behind as a form of torture."

Cornelia wanted to leave him behind so that she wouldn't be torturing herself. She needed distance, not closeness, to understand what was going on between them. Taking him to her bed had been a huge mistake...except it hadn't been and she didn't regret a second of it. But lacking time to even think about it was an increasing problem.

The President headed toward the door waving for Zachary and Daniel to join him.

They moved, leaving only her and Damien, who was still on the phone making arrangements.

At the threshold, the President paused and turned to her. Any sense of humor was gone. "Remember, specifically, to ask Pejman to communicate with his father-in-law and say 'What can be done to help with this gulf between us?' Word-for-word. 'Gulf between us'."

Cornelia nodded indicating that she had it.

The President nodded in return. "That should be of some assistance. Now get moving," and he was gone.

Damien, off the phone, held her coat for her. "There will be a car waiting by the time we get to the West Wing entrance."

Even a car wasn't going to get them there in time.

———

"You're Eddie?"

Damien loved it when Cornelia became flustered. It was very hard to do, so he decided to enjoy the occasion.

"Only two people call me that, not even my wife." General Arnson sounded grouchy about it, but then he sounded grouchy about everything as a matter of principle. "First was my nephew's wife. Then her best friend felt all put out that he was the Commander in Chief but Emily called me Eddie. The two are so competitive about everything."

But he smiled at Cornelia. The general almost never smiled.

"My apologies, General Arnson."

"No need, Ms. Day. No need. Finding myself partial to you. Need to log a little airtime myself and we have a Bell 505 Jet Ranger X that they gave us for testing." He waved at a very sleek helicopter, the only one not painted Marine Corps green. It was done in a bright, racy orange. "Time to put it through its paces. We'll have a car waiting for you at the other end."

"Actually, I think a taxi makes for a lower profile."

Damien saw the general register the level of trust she had given him. Not who she was meeting, but that it wasn't some whim that was taking her to New York either. There was a nicety to her communication.

"No car. Got it. You can sit up front with me. Leave this young whippersnapper who keeps sighing after you in the rear."

"Hey!"

"Or we can leave him behind altogether if you'd like."

Why was everyone threatening to do that to him today? Wasn't it enough how fast Cornelia was leaving him behind? Not that she was running away, but she did always seem to be three steps ahead, leaving him to catch up.

Rangers lead the way! and *Marines first to fight!*—neither branch had a clue. Because way out in front of them all was Chief of Staff Cornelia Day.

He did get the general aside for a moment.

"Sir, do you have a sidearm I could borrow?"

"Where's your piece?"

"In the safe at the Situation Room."

"Not doing you any damn good there, is it, Captain?"

"No sir."

"She going in alone?"

"Except for me."

"God help us," the general brushed aside the lapel of Damien's jacket and grunted his dissatisfaction at not finding a holster there.

Damien followed him to a gun safe in the private office. The general punched in a code and pulled out two-and-a-half pounds of a monster M1911, shoulder holster, and two spare magazines.

"You let her down one little inch, Mr. Librarian, and I'll have your Marine ass on the next ship to the Arabian Sea. Clear?"

"Yes, sir." Damien knew he meant it as well. It didn't matter that Damien was on the National Security Council and in an entirely different chain of command—he could deliver.

"Mount up," then the general nodded toward the big .45 in Damien's hands. "But hit the can first and strap on. Don't want her seeing that you're going in heavy. And I don't want some analyst pissing the back of my new helicopter."

"No, sir." By the time he saluted he was facing the general's back.

"Yeah, yeah," General Arnson replied as he walked away sounding like nothing so much as a Jewish grandfather.

For the whole flight up, Damien sat in the back and listened over the intercom while the kick-ass general chatted with Cornelia about her service with Zachary Thomas and even gave her a lesson in flying a helicopter. He spent the entire flight staring at the cartoonish Santa Claus some wag had taped to the back of Cornelia's seat.

6

"THIS IS WHERE MEG RYAN HAD HER FAKE ORGASM SCENE IN *When Harry Met Sally.*" Damien directed her attention across the street.

"Haven't seen that one," and Cornelia couldn't think of a single thing more irrelevant to the moment than a fake orgasm—there'd certainly been no need for that last night. The peaks had slammed through her so hard that she could still feel them.

The more she'd traveled on the way to Katz's, the stranger the experience had become.

Flying in the front of a helicopter for the first time had been fun and General Arnson's easy kindness had been a pleasant surprise—especially after her humiliating a whole section of his intelligence staff at dinner last night.

Starting her first ever visit to New York City by landing at the Downtown Manhattan Heliport had been a surreal element out of the movies; though the chilly wind off the East River made clear that it wasn't some glamour moment.

Somehow, in all of the years, she hadn't been a part of Zachary Thomas' trips here.

Now, after a taxi ride that had made DC drivers seem rational, she was staring at a neighborhood that made little sense. The street's four lanes were split by a median populated by struggling trees. A few construction barricades were decorated with brilliant graffiti. And several Salvation Army Santas with little steel donation buckets were ringing handbells.

"I bet only one of these is legit. The rest are just scammers," but Damien tucked a dollar or two into the bucket of each Santa they passed.

The four corners of the intersection they were dropped at had a genteel old six-story brick apartment building, a new twenty-story glass one, a park that there wasn't a chance she was going to enter without an armed guard, and a shabby-looking one-story wreck with big signs declaring it to be their destination. The neon sign spelled *Katz's Delicatessen,* but only because it was broad daylight; at night it would have spelled *Kat...'s D...e...n* because most of the bulbs were burned out. There was a painted sign, that really needed repainting, and—

"Are you serious about this? We flew all this way to come here?"

"Best Jewish deli there is. Boston? Feh. Tel Aviv? They've got no idea. Katz's is the place. Can you believe that they ship salamis all over the world to overseas service men and women from right here in lower Manhattan?" He took her hand and she let him lead her across the street.

It was the first time they'd touched since he'd caressed her behind while he'd still lay in her bed looking like a very smug demigod and she had stood stupidly over him, helpless at his merest caress. It had taken a brute-force will to leave his side. She'd had pretty lovers before, and not so pretty ones. But something about this Marine Corps captain could spoil her for life. So handsome and fit and sure of himself...that she wanted to jump him here and now.

He held the door for her and the warm air that washed over her brushed away all of her doubts and worries, at least about the meeting place. The air was so thick with smoked meats, chicken soup, and pickles that it was practically a meal unto itself.

Someone handed them each a ticket.

"Don't lose that."

Cornelia looked down at it, "Why? Are they raffling off a salami?"

"No, but they put your order on it. Fifty-dollar fee if you lose it."

She handed it to Damien. It was one too many things for her to deal with.

"What?"

"My phone is on my dresser and my tablet is on my desk at work. I'm losing too many things today." Like control of her life.

"Okay. Do you see him anywhere?"

"I don't even know what he looks like. Do you?"

"No. As soon as I saw his job, I rushed back to you. Besides this place is a zoo."

"Some help you are." But it was a zoo. Saturday afternoon the place was packed; it was actually a good place for an anonymous meeting, if they could ever find each other.

The main area was jammed with dozens of beige-and-battered Formica tables with equally unworthy wooden chairs.

A long deli counter ran down the entire length of the sidewall. Above the deli hung hundreds of different-sized salamis.

The non-deli walls were covered floor-to-ceiling with signed photographs. Some of them were bright and new, others appeared to date from the '20s and '30s. There was so much crazy decor, signs, and photographs covering the walls and dangling from the ceiling that she couldn't even focus on the crowds of people lined up at the counter and sniffing around for an open table, their hands filled with platters of massive sandwiches.

"We'll let him find us. He clearly remembers you. Food and sit."

So they ordered food. She remembered the President's request and ordered a pastrami to go and a corned beef for here. When she saw the size of the sandwiches, she wondered if she could even finish a half. Probably not even that, despite her crashing blood sugar, with the way her stomach was knotted.

Soon they were settled at a table with a vanilla New York egg cream, that Damien insisted was the best drink on earth, and a black-and-white cookie, oddly enough called a Black and White, that was nearly as big as her face.

"He should find us here," Damien waved upward with half of his Reuben sandwich.

She had to lean back to read the circular sign over their heads. *Where Harry met Sally...hope you had what she had! Enjoy!* with an arrow pointing directly to the top of her head.

"Nobody ever gets this table. It's a famous table. Usually people wait in line for it."

"For a table?"

"Sure. It's a superstar among furniture, the Meryl Streep of tables," he spoke around a mouthful of sandwich. "We'll watch the movie. You'll like it. Then you'll be glad that you're having what she had."

Cornelia waited until he was about to swallow. "Does that *having* include you?"

Damien coughed, choked, sputtered, then choked some more.

Cornelia took her first bite. It was good. Really good. She was half tempted to say so when she looked up and recognized a face in the crowd.

———

"Oh. My. God!"

"Good, isn't it? I told you it would be." Several sips of egg cream had managed to ease Damien's throat enough that an ambulance was no longer a desperate necessity. He'd have to remember to watch out for her sense of humor in the future.

Then he looked up at Cornelia's face. It had gone white as the DC snow.

He started to turn.

"No, don't!"

He faced back toward her, set down his sandwich, and eased his hand inside his jacket and around the butt of the M1911 pistol.

"Don't do that either, unless you want to get us shot."

So much for being subtle about traveling armed.

"I'm guessing that is President Javad Madani."

"Like the President of Iran? That Javad Madani?" Damien was suddenly very glad he wasn't eating because his mouth had gone dry way past the ability of an egg cream to fix.

"He's going to order. Shadowed by two guards. A fourth man is headed our way."

Damien managed to turn enough to see the backs of

three men approaching the sandwich counter. He recognized the walk of the two who were a step behind—military, well-trained military. Their suits weren't all that different from the Secret Service dudes. And they were watching the crowd, not studying the menu posted on the wall behind the counter.

"Ms. Day?" a man asked from close beside Damien's other elbow—some bodyguard he was turning out to be. The new arrival was in his early thirties and dressed in business casual. The accent was British-English, but with more dynamics—exactly as would be typical of a Farsi speaker.

"Mr. Pejman," Cornelia didn't ask.

"I am pleased that you were able to arrive. Our—my time, it is very limited. *I* am enroute between the UN and the airport. There is a flight that...uh, I must be on in two hours."

"Perhaps we should dispense with pretense and you should signal the rest of your party to join us." And the nervous Cornelia of this morning was gone in that instant.

Damien now sat across from the smoothly cool woman who had so captivated his attention on her first visit to the Situation Room and so thoroughly eviscerated his friends last night. Knowing some of what lay beneath only made her all the more dramatic and amazing.

At Pejman's signal, one of the guards did come to the table. He snapped out something in Farsi.

"Your bodyguard," Pejman translated, "may wait for us elsewhere."

"Actually," Damien had briefly considered hiding his knowledge, but then thought better of it. "This *'asshole'* has no intention of *'getting lost.'* He is very comfortable where he is." He took a bite of his sandwich and winked at Cornelia.

He could see by her sigh of relief that Farsi wasn't in her repertoire. It was almost a shock, discovering something she *couldn't* do.

"Without trust, there is no purpose," Cornelia began gathering her plate and the President's wrapped-to-go sandwich. "Come, Damien."

"I agree," a man said as he came up from the side of the table opposite Pejman.

Damien spun back the other way, reaching for his holster in surprise. Thankfully he managed to stop his hand before it arrived, the other guard already had his hand beneath his jacket and was watching him closely.

Beside the tall guard stood a small, dapper man with a graying beard and a neat suit. No tie, open collar. He looked like any of the myriad of other businessmen enjoying a casual lunch, except for the two guards probably less than a second from killing Damien.

He recognized President Javad Madani from his very rare Sit Room video calls.

Damien very slowly eased both of his hands hand to rest flat on the table.

The two guards relaxed only minimally.

"Yes," President Madani continued, observing the action. "Trust can be very difficult."

"Then perhaps," Cornelia remained in complete control, "you will send your guards off to get their own lunches while you join me with yours."

He studied her for a long moment, then told the guards to find some food and choose a table nearby but not too close. "And your guard?"

"He is..." and he could see that Cornelia did not know how to approach this. Marine, librarian, Situation Room intelligence officer: none of those would go well.

"I am a top advisor to Ms. Day."

"He's my most *trusted* advisor." Her smile and President Madani's nod of acceptance said that they'd cleared that hurdle.

"May Mr. Pejman join us as well?"

"As soon as you have your own lunches," again that perfect blend of courtesy and edge. *I am the one in control, but I can be kind.* It was a hell of a powerful, and sexy though he'd keep that to himself, message.

One of the guards delivered two plates and two drinks to the table and then retreated once more after giving Damien a foul look.

The other two men sat. Damien didn't like Pejman sitting next to Cornelia, but Damien had the seat across from her and the President had taken the one beside him, so whatever danger Pejman represented, Damien would be hard pressed to intervene quickly.

He was glad this was New York. A quick glance about the neighboring tables indicated that absolutely nothing out of the ordinary had been noticed. If something did happen, it was a city of fearless people, many armed with mace and Tasers. But the only people watching them were the two guards now carrying there own meals to an open spot three tables away where the sign above them said that Bill Clinton had eaten a whole pastrami sandwich, two hot dogs, fries, diet ginger ale, and a decaf coffee.

"Mr. Pejman," Cornelia turned to him. "I don't recall meeting you in Italy."

"My apologies, we did not. At least not directly. However, I observed that you were never far from your Vice President and I suggested that you might be an appropriate person with which to make contact. I was unaware of your promotion prior to my call. My congratulations."

"Thank you."

Damien almost laughed at the dryness of Cornelia's tone. Without it, she wouldn't be here and he wondered how much she was regretting her quick transition to power.

"Before I forget," Cornelia picked up without missing a beat. "Our President has asked me to request a message be passed on to your father-in-law."

Damien didn't miss Pejman's furtive glance across the table. Neither did Cornelia.

She turned to the President of Iran. "Mr. Pejman is married to your daughter."

"He makes her happy. And he will be a powerful man someday, if he remains smart."

Pejman tried to sit up straighter than he already was.

"Then my message must be for you: 'What can be done to help with this gulf between us?' I assume this means more than it appears to."

Damien had missed the President saying that. He'd been...oh, on the phone worrying about logistics of getting here. He should also have been listening for what they were supposed to do once they had.

President Madani truly smiled for the first time. "I was skeptical of my son-in-law's suggestion of meeting with a woman, Ms. Day. But I see now that you are strong and intelligent like my daughter. Forgive me, but our culture creates expectations that are difficult to surmount."

Damien would have asked for the hidden meaning of the phrase, now that he understood there was one, but Cornelia didn't. She knew something. No, she knew no more than he did.

Therefore she had concluded...what?

That President Matthews was confirming a past relationship and letting Madani know that Cornelia had the

American President's stamp of approval; no other information was relevant.

"However," Madani's mood lightened, "digestion does not go well with such topics. Tell me, Ms. Day, are you married?" And he picked up his own sandwich.

———

CORNELIA MAINTAINED THE CONVERSATION AS WELL AS SHE could. Small talk was not one of her strengths, especially not with everything else that was occupying her thoughts. *The gulf between us?*

Perhaps *the* Gulf...

The Persian Gulf?

But that wasn't *between* them.

Her role was also rather mystifying.

She had thought she'd had some grasp of what her duties as White House Chief of Staff were. Those duties didn't have anything to do with a brigadier general acting as her personal pilot, currently cooling his heels at a Manhattan heliport, while she ate a corned beef sandwich with a foreign head of state—an aggressively non-allied one.

They also didn't involve having her ankles wrapped around Damien's under the table while doing so. She hadn't even been aware of it until this moment. She certainly was not going to think about him or what they had done last night; not while they sat in a New York Jewish deli discussing Javad Madani's grandchildren.

"When in the course of human events..." Madani's tone didn't change.

That wasn't what alerted her to the sudden shift in the conversation. It was Damien's ankles twitching against hers.

"...it becomes necessary for people of good will to come together over good food."

He'd opened with the first line of the Declaration of Independence, mostly. He'd paused. Waiting for...? Her answer!

"We the people..." she finally countered with the Constitution, but not *of the United States,* "...of global good will, must indeed come together."

"However carefully," President Madani countered.

"However carefully," she nodded to include that they were having a secret meeting in the middle of a busy deli.

"This time the storm enters from the Bay, not the Gulf."

Cornelia could hear the capitalized words in his soft speech. She struggled for the meaning. *The Gulf between us.* What if that was the Gulf of Mexico?

The storm.

Not Hurricane Katrina.

A different kind of storm. One involving Iran and the United States.

The storm of...an attack! There must have been plans for an attack on the United States to which Iran's President was not only privy, but perhaps essential in preventing.

And the Bay? New York? New York had Upper and Lower New York Bay, but other than the Statue of Liberty, it would be an attack on Staten Island or Brooklyn, not Manhattan proper.

"Nobody hates Brooklyn that much, though not true-blue New Yorker would miss Staten Island for a heartbeat." At Damien's whispered remark, Cornelia decided perhaps the city wasn't the target despite having two bays.

Washington, DC, however, most certainly had a very prominent one: the Chesapeake.

Did this whole conversation have to occur in code? She

hoped not. But clearly the first part must be, unless it was a test of some sort. Or a precaution.

She glanced over at the two guards still watching them carefully from their table.

Damien followed her gaze then nodded. "You have well-trained men, Mr. President. Their attention to duty doesn't waver with time or a good meal," he waved genially to their own empty plates.

He was clearly saying it for her benefit.

Madani has brought his most trusted men, Damien was telling her, *but not trusted enough to tell them who he was meeting with.* If the guards knew that she and Damien were from the White House, she suspected that they would either be more relaxed or far more suspicious rather than merely watchful.

President Madani had asked for this meeting.

President Matthews had said, *What can be done to help with this gulf between us?*

Was President Madani seeking or offering help?

"I am here," she was still struggling to connect the pieces. "Rather than...my superior, as normal channels are not...always careful enough."

The President remained silent, not correcting her. Not until she made a mistake? If she did, then what? Ballistic missiles raining down from space? Iran was one of the select nations that could launch them. No. Or they wouldn't be here.

"Does this...friendly conversation have one side or two?" She had better not be in the middle of a quid pro quo conversation with the twelfth most powerful nation in the world. And she'd wager that they held their cards even closer than North Korea and that in reality they were a few notches higher than twelfth. Perhaps no one was willing to deliver the bad news to the American allies of Canada or South Korea at Ten and Eleven.

"No conversation," Madani corrected, "in our modern global economy can risk having only one side."

She was going to strangle President Matthews for putting her into this situation. Perhaps not her best idea, as that would result in a charge of treason and a life's sentence. Maybe she'd...throw away his pastrami sandwich. *You go, girl! That'll show him.*

Cornelia took a careful breath.

As if knowing her utter loss of how to continue, Madani spoke once more. "But for now, let us speak only of how I may be a friend to you on this one occasion."

"Bless you!"

He nodded his head at her vast relief. "We have learned, by methods I believe inappropriate for a woman to know, that there is an attack coming. It is neither chemical nor biological. I am informed, with no further clarity, that it is cultural."

"Cultural. In DC."

Damien could only offer her a shrug. Madani offered no reaction at all.

Cornelia decided her best option was to wait, especially as she didn't know how to take the next step.

"When we are teaching our young the prayers of a true believer, we often tell them: you must pray with your heart, not your words."

"You are saying I should take up prayer from my heart?"

Madani smiled tolerantly. "I can think of little better advice, but that was not my point."

"This...person," Pejman spoke with disgust, "spoke his final words as a child. Repeating them until they were past any meaning. He said: *We shall cut out their heart with their own words.*" They were the first words Pejman had spoken since making introductions. He had seemed but a passive go-between until this moment. But his evident fury and what sounded like personal experience made him into a suddenly menacing and dangerous man who had overseen the questioning and confession of a man now dead.

"My apologies for my son-in-law. He is a very passionate man." And with those words, President Madani dropped his napkin on his plate and rose to his feet.

"You have no more for us?" Cornelia cursed herself the moment she'd said it. If he did, he'd have offered it already.

"I can only offer you my prayers during this, your Christian holiday season." Madani pressed his palms together briefly and then, after only a moment's hesitation, reached across to shake her hand.

His clasp was firm but brief.

"You are the first woman I have touched other than my wife and daughter since the day of my wedding."

"I will take that as a blessing."

"Take it as a statement that if your *most-trusted advisor* does not have the common sense that Allah gave an elephant, I shall speak to my wife about my taking a second one."

When he shook Damien's hand, without the hesitation, Damien spoke cheerfully as if to a friend. "Don't lose your food tickets."

"It is not my first trip to Katz's," the President laughed.

Damien retained the President's hand a moment longer, "And I do have more common sense than God gave a horse."

"Good. Then I shall call you friend and you shall bring your wife to meet mine when you come to visit us." He turned for the door and his guards fell into place beside him.

Pejman did not presume to shake her hand, but did shake Damien's as he spoke to her.

"My thanks, Ms. Day." She felt that he managed his exit line without choking on it too badly.

"Pending doom. This is *really* not how I was thinking this Saturday was going to turn out," she wanted to collapse at the table and fake something. Like a belief that everything was going to be okay.

Damien held out her coat. "So, that was fun. Who are we meeting with next? The Chinese Paramount Leader at Barney's for bagels and lox about a war in the South China Sea? Then uptown to Zabar's for gefilte fish with the Russian Prime Minister to find out how soon his submarines are going to attack the East Coast? Seriously I need to hang out with you more often. I can't wait until we meet the real Santa Claus."

"You're Jewish," though she appreciated his attempts at levity.

"Technically," he gathered her to-go sandwich for the President, offered her his arm, and escorted her toward the door.

An elderly couple pounced on their table before they were two steps away.

"But I still have more common sense than God gave a horse, no matter which God he is."

"Or she."

"Or she," he agreed as he paid for their two tickets.

Cornelia had lost all ability to think. Definitely to think about President Madani's departing benediction.

But his indefinite hints at terrorist attacks was scaring the daylights out of her.

7

"AND THAT'S ALL HE SAID?"

Damien could only nod. He didn't dare look at the Sit Room clock. Who knew how many hours they'd been here. He'd intentionally sat with his back to the big digital displays that showed local and President time. They'd be in sync right now because the President was sitting at the head of the table, but Damien didn't want to know.

He'd never so appreciated his anonymous role at the duty watch officer's desk. Or so wanted to get back to it.

For the entire flight home in the back of the helicopter, they'd written down every word they could remember—even the during meal chat about families. After checking with him on a scribbled note, Cornelia had used General Arnson as a sounding board to force them to remember as much as possible. Then all three of them had been whisked into the Situation Room. An ever-changing array of senior staff had arrived, questioned, departed, returned...

Someone served them a late dinner he couldn't recall, but the whirlwind didn't slow—it grew. The President, the Gentlemen Elect, Sienna the National Security Advisor,

General Brett Rogers, Chairman of the Joint Chiefs of Staff, and too many others for him to keep track of were called in until there wasn't an empty seat and there were plenty more standing: Homeland Security, counter-terrorism, Secret Service...

A cultural attack.

Perhaps during: *your Christian holiday season.*

We shall cut out their heart with their own words.

Though it was Saturday afternoon, substitute copies of the Declaration and Constitution had been put on display and the originals placed in the main vault at the National Archives. That President Madani had opened his conversation with the first line of the Declaration had been too much for even the skeptics to dismiss.

Beyond that, it was generally agreed that unless President Madani could offer them some further details at a later time, there was little that could be surmised or done.

Still they had talked.

And talked.

And talked.

He and Cornelia had been asked questions until they were wrung dry—every word, every nuance questioned and re-questioned. Even Cornelia's perfect posture was finally sagging.

That's what finally kicked him into action. That fact that Cornelia was less than her incredible self was so wrong that it dragged him from his own pending stupefaction.

"We're done," his voice came out as little more than a croak.

When no one paid any attention to him, he rose to his feet, and managed to find a little more volume.

"We're done."

Still no effect.

So he took Cornelia's hand in his and helped her to her feet. He could feel her shaking. Over everyone's sudden protests, he simply led her from the room.

Damien forgot to look away from the wall clock as he passed by it: oh-seven-hundred.

Twenty-four hours. They'd been on the go for twenty-four straight hours, fourteen of them in this goddamn room.

Leading her by the hand, they passed by the watch desk.

Marko's low whistle of surprise was the only sound from his team, who were getting a start-of-shift briefing from the prior team. He glanced over at them.

Felice and Vaccaro both gave him a thumbs-up, and Caron whispered softly, "Bugger me! The Chief of Staff? Good on ya, mate."

Cornelia was stumbling worse than a drunk as he led her out into the White House foyer. The dawn was still lost somewhere behind freshly dark clouds.

"I have a car and driver waiting for you," the head of the President's Secret Service detail, Frank Adams, loomed up beside him. He handed them their coats. Damien had forgotten to grab them, which told him how poorly he himself was functioning.

"You're the best, Frank."

"No, that's my wife. But thanks for saying it. You take care of this lady."

"Already on it."

"I see that," he glanced down at their joined hands.

"Go to hell, Frank."

"Bound to, Damien. Good morning, Ms. Day," he saw them all the way to the car and personally closed the door behind them.

She was asleep on Damien's shoulder by the time they reached her condo.

The morning doorman, who'd given him nothing but the evil eye at this time yesterday, rushed to hold the door as he carried her in. She curled up in his arms like a lover. Her head on his shoulder, her arms draped about his neck. She weighed nothing, as if her exhaustion was so deep that all substance had been dragged from her.

There was enough light through her east-facing windows, despite the glowering sky, that Damien could navigate her apartment. He lay her down atop the rose-colored comforter on the bed, he pulled off her boots, then sat down in a floral armchair for a moment to gather the energy to take off her coat and tuck her in.

It was the last thing he remembered.

8

————

COLD.

Cornelia reached for the blanket. She wasn't under one.

Still cold.

She was lying down in her coat, on her bed. The pillow smelled of...

Damien! Where was—

She opened her eyes to the room, and had to squint. The heavy overcast sky still let too much light in the two tall windows that faced the park across the street. Once she grew accustomed to the brightness, she spotted him. He too still wore his coat, slouched in the chair by her dresser. Through the uncurtained windows, the day looked icy cold against the dark gray sky—sleeting rain slapped against the glass in hard gusts.

Damien slept as if he'd been cut down in place. His arms hanging off either side of the chair, his head tipped sideways as if some headsman had done only a mediocre job of chopping him off at the neck.

He didn't look much like a conquering hero, but he was. She remembered how strong and steady he'd been through the endless debriefing. She'd never have made it as long as she did without his constant encouragement.

And then he'd rescued her.

It was a moment that maidens in distress were supposed to recall and she didn't know whether she was happy or sad that she mostly didn't. She'd never been so tired in her life. Then his hand had lifted her from her seat and she'd been whisked away in some fairy carriage that had felt like being held in his arms. And had woken up—

Cold.

Cornelia managed to regain her feet and stumbled over her leather Blondo mid-calf boots she'd chosen yesterday. They'd have been more useful if they were still on her feet. Pulling her coat more tightly about her didn't decrease the chill, neither did rubbing her feet together—two chafing icicles, not body warmth. She moved around the room, dropping the curtains into place, shutting out the too bright morning. She didn't know what time she gotten into, or at least onto her bed, but it hadn't been long enough ago.

When she passed by Damien, she jostled his arm.

"Huh?" No more than an incoherent grunt. Then a groan as he tried to straighten out his neck.

She jostled him again, "Into the bed, now."

He looked up at her, over at the bed, down at himself— at least he still wore his boots—then back up at her. "Huh?"

Cornelia decided that he was awake enough to figure out the next steps for himself. She shed her coat, and clothes over the other armchair and felt terribly bohemian for not hanging them up. Slipping on a flannel nightgown, she then crawled back under the covers and pulled them over her head.

She could hear Damien stumble to his feet. After a few miscellaneous and manly grunts, he slid naked beneath the covers. Is this what it would be like to live with a man? She'd never done that, never shared her living space except for a night here and there. Which was all she'd done with Damien. So why was she suddenly thinking what it would be like to live with the man?

He slipped a hand out in the darkness, found her breast, whispered a "sorry," then slid his hand about her waist and pulled her in as if she weighed nothing.

One thing for sure, living with a man was a much warmer option. Ignoring propriety, she rolled over and plastered herself against him: her twined arms and hands trapped between them, her legs slipping between his, her face burrowed against his shoulder.

"Well, good morning," she liked the deep rumble of his chest and pushed harder against it. How could a person be so deliciously warm? Would that be a problem in the hot summer? No, she had air conditioning. It would still be incredible.

"Go back to sleep. We need sleep," Cornelia could feel it dragging at her very bones.

"Fat chance," he pulled her in tighter until he was practically crushing her against him.

"So warm," her fingers must feel like ice against his warm chest, but he didn't complain.

"Is that all I am to you? A life-sized heating unit?"

"Absolutely."

He shifted to slide his other arm beneath her head and his powerful biceps became her pillow.

"Very warm. Very nice." And so male that she wondered what that made her prior lovers. Technically male, but they had been political and office types. Damien might work as a librarian in the Situation Room, but Marine radiated off him.

He kissed her on top of the head and she did her best not to purr.

She huddled inside his embrace and soaked up the warmth and the wonder of his embrace. The wonder of it, that was the biggest surprise. Damien didn't hold or hug her, he embraced her. He held her the same way he looked at her, as if she was more important than anything.

The sensation stilled her thoughts and quieted her soul until she was aware of only two things: Damien's warmth and his luscious smell.

———

"How in the world can you fall asleep like this?" Damien kept his question silent so that he didn't wake Cornelia.

Her flannel nightgown hid nothing, wrapping her in a second, plush skin. From her freezing toes pressed tight atop his own to her soft hair tucked under his chin, there wasn't a single point not in contact.

She was asleep.

His body was vibrant with need. He ached to touch, taste, feel, enter.

And she was asleep.

A power ran through him, the like of which he'd rarely felt since his six months in the Marine Corps officer training at The Basic School at Quantico. It was the course that made four years of NROTC and the three summers between look like a lazy-assed cakewalk. For six months he'd done everything from rifle platoon tactics and crew-served weapons—the Marines loved their howitzers and missile launchers—to signals intelligence and ground electronic warfare.

At the end of The Basic School a Marine either became an officer or became an officer—Marines never quit. But that didn't mean it was easy or that all graduates were created equal. Screw up and a Marine didn't get a choice on where he landed —*infantry command here I come.* Graduate at the top, talk nice to the intelligence instructors, do a tour at Marine Intel, and get recommended straight into National Security Council.

He'd done it right: every single goddamn step of it for four years of school, a half more at Quantico, and every training course since.

The toughest instructor of them all had been the NSC's prior senior watch officer. Damien's first two-year tour at the watch desk had been pure hell and Laslow had made sure of it. Every lousy, impossible, bound-to-come-apart-at-exactly-the-wrong-moment job had somehow landed on his desk.

He knew Laslow was behind it, but Damien had survived enough Marine Corps instructors that an asshole Defense Intelligence Agency liaison wasn't going to get to him.

Then, when his tour was up, he was reassigned to the Sit Room—which never happened. After two more years of Laslow hell, the man had taken him aside.

"You're it, Feinman. You're in again, but I'm out. You disappoint me and I'm going to come back from the grave to haunt you."

"You planning on dying?" The man had been at least seventy even back then—and sharp as hell.

"Wife's got family in Louisiana. I *hate* Louisiana. Dying will be a goddamn blessing."

Last Damien had heard, he was playing in the winning money of senior golf tournaments.

Damien had taken over, providing continuity to the NSC

watch team for three more tours since. Any Marine up on the line who said Damien hadn't earned his captain's bars could go suck on a hot howitzer barrel. Once he'd made it, Damien had *known* how strong he was.

Or thought he had.

All that had been blown away by the strength he felt holding onto the woman in his arms.

Cornelia wasn't weak, not a single ounce of her. But still he felt truly strong in this moment, protecting her from the world.

Focus on the moment! Laslow had yelled at him.

Damien was always thinking about future strategy and possibilities. How to better advise the very top policy makers.

It was a variation of the tirade that Cornelia had unleashed on his Marine Intel buddies. His thinking didn't need to remain tactical, as theirs did. Instead, it needed to be focused on what was needed at the moment—*and to anticipate the next.* He like to think of it as: the Feinman Corollary to the Laslow Initiative.

That's what Damien had striven to teach the teams since he'd taken over as the leader of the duty watch. To serve the room in the very best way, it was always necessary to think about the next moment. To anticipate it. To have the information ready before they asked for it.

Sometimes the effort was wasted, when the question never came or conversation veered in another direction. But it had forced the watch team to bring a new level to their game.

And what Cornelia needed right now was sleep.

He knew that.

No matter what he needed. She—

"How much longer are you going to lie there thinking so hard?" Her voice whispered against his chest.

"You're asleep." He'd known she was asleep. She still wasn't moving a single muscle.

"Uh-huh. Clearly. And if you try to hold me any harder, our bodies will merge and become one."

"Oh, sorry," but he couldn't bring himself to ease off. All of his protective thoughts were still keeping her clasped tightly against him. "Letting you go doesn't appear to be an option."

"Good. Don't."

And she shifted ever so slowly. Sliding from huddled warmth inside the protective circle of his arms, to a lover holding him as well.

By the time he slipped the flannel nightgown off her, her breath was no longer so calm and steady.

When he finally rolled her onto her back, it was short and choppy with rough gasps.

And when the ultimate release rocked through both their bodies, he didn't feel merely strong, he felt triumphant.

9

AFTER ANOTHER FOUR HOURS OF SLEEP AND THEN DELIVERY Chinese food, Damien had slid back to sleep. But that escape eluded Cornelia.

Ultimately she wasn't going to solve anything lying next to Damien while he slept. Half an hour later she sat at her desk in the West Wing. Nearing midnight on a Sunday night, there was no one to disturb her thought processes. Or her body. *Disturbing* her body? She wasn't some sacrosanct temple. Damien wasn't disturbing her body, he was messing with her emotional balance.

She sighed and pushed back from her computer before she even got started. It was clear that she wasn't going to find a way to compartmentalize Damien Feinman unless she assigned him some concentrated thought.

Then she pulled herself back to the computer because thinking about Damien was a one-way road. If she was going to go back to thinking about her fantasy lover—he wasn't the only one allowed to have happy fantasies—then she might as well have stayed in bed with him.

How could he even think she was asleep? She could feel

his thoughts churning away almost as strongly as his arms had been embracing her. No man ever held a woman that way.

She was used to...compromising. It was a sad statement on her past, but it was true. Damien had certainly spoiled her for average men. Whenever this ended, she was going to mourn the loss, and then become a nun and take a vow of celibacy so that she could concentrate on her work once more.

First she pulled up the latest from the NSC.

Only two things in the queue, starting with the report of her own interview. She ran through it, making little more than a few proofing marks. The last lines stumped her, they were not what she had reported. Cornelia's version had included that they were invited to visit Tehran as a guest of the President.

But this version included the entire exchange about President Madani's complimentary mock proposal to her, Damien's statement about having common sense, and Madani's invitation to Damien *and his wife.* She knew she hadn't said that in any of the debriefings—she'd been very careful not to even think about that, never mind say it aloud.

And it wasn't word for word, so it couldn't have been a clandestine recording arranged without her knowledge. It must have been from Damien. *Him* she could kill. Perhaps not President Matthews for placing her in the center of this mess in the first place, but any compunction she might have had about committing bodily harm on the NSC librarian had gone out the window.

Didn't he understand who would see this report? It was already far more obvious than she would like that they were having a relationship. Then she remembered him holding her hand as he led her from the Sit Room this morning.

He'd done that in front of her current boss and her future one.

She'd now flaunted it in front of the President and the President-elect—never mind the NSA, the Joint Chiefs of Staff, General Arnson, and Damien's own staff—that she was sleeping with a man she'd known barely a week. Worse, with someone who had made what now amounted to a public declaration that he could envision them married.

This was spiraling out of control and it was time to end it.

When he came in, this morning, she would call him into her office and simply announce that it was over. She would miss him. The incredible sex, the charming companionship, and the way he held her—she'd especially miss that—but she had to be practical and get her life back under her own control.

No need to make a note on her to-do list, she wouldn't forget.

That aspect of her life resolved, she digitally signed the stupid memo—with its ludicrous happy-ever-after statement—as being reasonably complete and adequately accurate. She'd learned to stop fighting that battle years ago. The only way to guarantee completely cogent reporting was to write it herself and there was never enough time for her to do both that and her job.

Good enough, moving on!

The second item in the NSC queue for her attention was the action report from yesterday's meetings.

There was the usual batch of naysayers, denying that an *enemy* country might ever reach out to help. Instead, it was purported, the Iranians must be instigating panic as a distraction from whatever their true purpose might be.

Follows: gross speculation and wild conjecture.

Cornelia skipped that section.

The President's response, included in the memo, had been less than kind in the words he'd used.

The catch was that those who did believe in President Madani's willingness to help hadn't been able to make any more sense of his warning than she and Damien had.

Then, there'd been a debate on how to prepare for an unknown threat at an unknown time. The NSA and CIA reported no increased chatter on suspected terrorist networks or known terrorist phones. Had they simply become wiser in their communications or were there really no communications to hear?

She went back to Madani's warning itself. Not a *gulf* this time, but *bay*. She reviewed his words carefully. He hadn't said DC, she was the one who had jumped to that conclusion. Madani hadn't denied that conclusion, but neither had he confirmed it. Was there some question? Had he shrugged uncertainly? She couldn't recall.

———

DAMIEN'S DESK PHONE RANG. HIS SHIFT WAS STILL FIVE HOURS away, but that didn't mean much when there was a crisis in the Sit Room and he'd come into work after waking alone. What was it about their schedules that kept leaving him in Cornelia's bed without Cornelia?

Maybe he should try taking her to his place. It was out in Tenleytown, but with the Metro, it wouldn't take much longer to reach the White House than walking from her Georgetown condo. Maybe he could keep her in his bed with more success than he'd kept her in her own. And maybe he could get a fresh change of clothes, he was currently wearing the emergency set he kept here at the White House.

"You planning on answering that?" Bettani was also in early. He'd sort of blocked out the phone. Some memory was itching at him and he hadn't found it yet.

"Damien," he didn't even look at the caller ID as he answered.

"Bay. He didn't say which bay," Cornelia's idea of a *Good morning, lover* moment—at least when she was in Chief of Staff mode.

"That's it!" Damien jolted upright in his chair. "That's what was bothering me. Thanks, you just saved me a world of heavy thinking."

"I've been doing it for hours," she sounded weary of it, but also energized. Her mind was awake, even if she must be physically exhausted.

"Come on down and we'll look at it."

There was a long pause that puzzled him. She sounded a little resigned when she said that she'd be down in a moment.

Damien shifted to the Briefing Room itself. He shut down the room's microphone, so that he wouldn't disturb the duty watch—he could do his own damn searches.

Cornelia joined him soon enough, but she didn't sit. Instead she came into the room and stopped, standing still and looking at him.

"How do you look so amazing at three in the morning?" Her attire reminded him simultaneously of the woman and the lover. Her tailored suit was impeccably professional—not unisex by any means, but alone it would have made no statement beyond *feminine.* However, around her collar she wore a brilliant red scarf of some flimsy material that added a flair that she didn't normally show. A flair that reminded him of the stunningly sensual woman who presented a neatly professional demeanor.

The look on her face at his compliment wasn't what he'd anticipated. No happy smile, not even the small quirk of one. Instead she was studying him with all the enthusiasm she might study a report on the latest requisition for a US Coast Guard ice breaker.

"There are over a hundred significant bays around the continental US." He decided that directing her attention to the screen was probably the safest choice at the moment. "Probably ten times that if we look at Alaska and Hawaii."

She moved slowly to the first seat on the left-hand side of the table and sat across from him. But she didn't look at him, instead inspecting the map of the US that he'd put up on one screen and a USGS list of bays on another. Cornelia didn't say anything about what was on her mind.

"I think," he struggled not to ask what the hell was going on, "that President Madani meant Chesapeake Bay, but we don't know that for sure. And from what I can remember, he wasn't sure either. So let's look at major bays and how they might relate to: *We shall cut out their heart with their own words.*"

Cornelia nodded, "Also, it would have to be a significant attack, with meaning. A terrorist wants everything to be showy."

"So Seattle Public Library would be out even though it sits only five blocks above Elliot Bay."

"Why are we starting at the bottom of the alphabet—Washington State?"

"I always do that, though I'm not sure why," Damien puzzled at it for a moment. "I think that it forces me to adopt a fresh view. Looking at everything backwards."

Cornelia glanced his way for a moment at that, then nodded for him to continue.

State by state they rolled up the list.

"I've always been partial to Depoe Bay in Oregon," he told her when they got to Oregon.

"Why? It's tiny."

"It's the smallest navigable bay in the world, at least according to the locals. They have a fishing fleet, and I use the word loosely, of less than a dozen craft. That plus a couple of whale watching boats."

"Not a likely target," Cornelia pointed out.

"Didn't say it was. Just said I was partial to it."

Cornelia covered her face with her hands for a moment. He wasn't sure if she was trying to hide a smile, or was about to go looking for a gun.

When she did neither, he continued.

New York was mostly a Harbor made up of two rivers, but they left it starred for consideration.

Long Island was a sound.

Massachusetts Bay outside of Boston was another maybe.

The Chesapeake still ranked as a most likely.

Maine had hundreds of bays along its craggy shores, but who could possibly care unless they lived there.

Hawaii seemed too remote to feel threatening, as did Alaska.

By the time they were done they had added only San Francisco and Delaware Bays—and the only interesting thing up the latter was Philadelphia and it wasn't technically on the bay, but rather on the river above that. Of course, DC wasn't on the Chesapeake either, but rather up the Potomac River from the bay.

"Are we overthinking this?" She asked when they had

their list of bays down to just three. "Are we putting too much emphasis on the word *bay?*"

Damien didn't know. "It's about all we have to go on."

"All we have to go on," Cornelia sighed.

Damien had often been accused of being a little oblivious when it came to women. Bettani or Marko were always telling him that he was missing all the signals, both the *Come here, boy* and the *It's about to be over!*

Not this time.

He heard Cornelia's subject change loud and clear.

"All we have to go on?" he prompted her cautiously. Just because he heard the subject change, didn't mean he had a clue what the new topic was.

"Damien," her tone sounded dire and she was looking at her folded hands, not the screen or him.

Her hands, that he so enjoyed looking at, even when he wasn't thinking about the incredible sensations they could draw from his body, were clenched together bloodlessly white.

"We—"

"Nope!" Damien cut her off.

"What do you mean?" That forced her gaze up to study him.

"I mean that if you're thinking about what I think you're thinking about, don't think about it because you're completely wrong."

"That didn't make any sense."

"It did when I said it," he puzzled over his own words for a moment. "Though perhaps less so when they came out."

"What are you saying?"

"I'm saying..." And he was about to put his foot in it, but he was afraid of what she'd say if he let her have the initiative. "I'm saying that if you're thinking about me not falling in love with you, you're already too late." Which sure as hell wasn't anything he'd meant to say.

———

CORNELIA COULD FEEL THE SILENCE SLIDE OVER HER. THAT cold clear wash of Vulcanesque logic that she had cultivated as a little girl. The one that had made her the most deadly debater at Claremont McKenna—a school known for its debate-style instruction. The one that she used when faced by unfriendly congressmen or demonstrably overly-friendly congressional aides.

Cut it off! Lock it away! Be safe!

None of that garbage out there was about her. She was safe inside herself. Safe from…

Damien watched her carefully across the President's Briefing Room table. He looked as surprised by what he'd said as she felt—if she was letting herself feel.

Which she wasn't.

But she did.

Feelings that she wanted to deny as impossible, except they were his feelings.

You can never simply know *what someone else is thinking. Your job is to find out.* It was one of Zachary Thomas' favorite sayings.

"I think I just found out."

"Found out what?" Damien asked softly. His deep voice sounded as if it was being strangled somewhere deep in his chest.

"That you're feeling what—" Cornelia couldn't quite bring herself to say it. "you say your feeling."

"I seem to." He dragged a hand through his hair, mussing it completely. It was one of his more endearing habits. "It's surprising the crap out of me if that's any comfort."

"Actually, it is."

"You—"

"Nope," she cut *him* off this time. "Don't give me any clichés about my not having to respond or if the next line isn't obvious or any of that."

"Okay," he shrugged and offered one of his smiles. "I'll just wait you out then."

"It may be a long wait, Damien."

"The President of Iran didn't seem to think so."

"He is also arrogantly male. He practically proposed to me over a pastrami sandwich."

"Corned beef."

"What?"

"I had a Reuben. You and President Madani had corned beef. Pejman was the one with pastrami and he didn't propose to you."

"As I said, arrogantly male," but she was having trouble hiding her smile.

"Something one arrogant male can appreciate in another."

"And on what do you base your own arrogance other than being a Marine?"

"And a librarian. Makes me a pretty special guy." Then he leaned forward as much as the table would reasonably allow. "But do you want to know the real reason?"

"I think that the answer to that would be no." Cornelia could feel her magnetic, unthinking, purely emotional draw to him and didn't like it. Actually, she did like it and that was even more unnerving.

"I figured, but I'll tell you anyway. The real, heretofore

unexpressed reason I feel so comfortable with being an arrogant male is quite simple."

"What's that?"

He reached out and rested one of his big strong hands over her clasped ones, enveloping them both with his warmth and power.

"See? I knew that you really wanted to know. But it's a secret," he whispered.

"We are in the Sit Room," and her smile did escape her control at his laugh.

"Lean closer and I'll whisper it."

Even as she told herself that wasn't going to happen, her body decided otherwise and she leaned in.

"I'm the guy who gets to tell Cornelia Day that he loves her." Then he leaned back and returned his voice to normal as if it was too much even for him. "If that isn't an excuse for unremitting arrogance, I don't know what is."

"Males," Sienna spoke from the doorway, "don't need an excuse to be arrogant. But what was yours? I couldn't quite hear it." She continued into the room and dropped her files at the chair beside Cornelia.

"I—"

"Any doubts," Sienna talked right over Cornelia's attempts to protest, "go up to the roof and ask my Secret Service sniper fiancé. That man actually thinks I'm going to happily marry him, bear his children, and grow old together."

"You aren't?" Cornelia couldn't hold back her surprise. They were so obviously in love.

"Oh, I am. Christmas Day. You're both invited if I didn't remember to send you invitations. Not a chance am I going to let a man that good out of my sights. But I'm not going to tell him that just because I said 'yes' when he proposed, all the rest of it is true."

"But—"

"So," Sienna kept talking. "Anything new to report, other than the obvious?" She nodded toward where Damien sat with a perplexed look on his face.

Cornelia managed to control her voice. Less sure of her hands, she slipped them out from under Damien's grasp and tucked them in her lap under the edge of the table. "Unless terrorists are going to be attacking the world's smallest fishing fleet harbor, we're still thinking that the Chesapeake is our primary candidate."

"Darn it! I didn't even think about the target *not* being DC. I need to get my head fixed."

"Actually," Cornelia couldn't help but feel a little envious of Sienna's clarity of thought and awareness of her own emotions, "your head seems like it's just fine to me."

Cornelia risked a glance over at Damien, but he was once again concentrating on the screen as if to verify their conclusions. It was hard not to wish that she too could talk about Damien with such heartfelt passion.

She almost laughed at that.

She had not just thought about being able to say such things about *someone,* she'd targeted Damien. Perhaps she did need to keep her overly logical thoughts to herself and simply give her *human-half* feelings time to be recognized. As she watched Damien work, she suspected that she knew what those feelings would be when they finally crystallized.

And for some reason, that wasn't worrying her nearly as much as she thought it should.

10

A WEEK OF TIME HADN'T SHED A SINGLE BIT OF LIGHT ON President Javad Madani's cryptic warning.

Damien had listened to scores of theories proposed and shot down during multiple Sit Room meetings. He'd done his best to migrate back to his watch desk, and had succeeded for the most part.

But he was still drawn into a much higher percentage of meetings than was usual for a man in his position. He tried not to read too much into it.

He liked his role as Sit Room librarian, the one person most deeply steeped in the knowledge of not only the room's operation, but also the history of the decisions which had been made here. He pre-dated the current administration despite their double term of office, and he had some hope of post-dating the next one even if they won a double term.

But their *Christian holiday season* was now a week shorter than it had been when Madani delivered his warning. The sense of impending disaster lurked in the corners of the room while meetings were held on other topics as well.

Then, the lurking shadow would crawl back into the open and knock the cheer out of any task, no matter how successfully done.

One thing had changed though. He'd now known Cornelia Day for two weeks rather than one. He gathered his coat and headed up the stairs and along the hall to her office.

Friday night. A week ago he'd invited her to Molly Malone's Pub for dinner. A week ago they'd slept together for the first time...though it felt as if they always had.

A lot had changed between them. He was even crazier about her than he had been. Her poise ran soul deep. She was the one who always lent the calmest voice to any meeting. When the unflappable President was ready to pound his fist through the face of some conniving South American ambassador, it was Cornelia who calmed the situation. Her chill poise was often enough to convince her *opponent* that their lives would be far less challenging if they were to cooperate...fully...and right now!

Gods but she tickled him no end.

Janet waved as he entered her office, and pointed to a chair while she continued on the phone. Usually this late in the day, Janet was gone and he could simply stick his head in to see if Cornelia was ready to go or if he should order in dinner. Something must be up beyond her cracked open door.

Janet, who looked like everybody's favorite grandmother, finished handing out a set of instructions on the phone. "I do care, dear. I care that the Chief of Staff has your report on her desk by six a.m. Monday morning....Yes, I understand that it is Friday night. However, the request was issued to your office on Tuesday and you know and I know that was plenty of warning. Now you must get it done or you will have to face me and then Ms. Day, and you know which will be the worse... Good!" And she hung up with more force than he expected from such a mild-mannered woman.

"Remind me never to make you mad, Janet." The threat of unleashing Cornelia's ire would be a great motivator for any man.

"That Secretary of the Interior. He is always doing everything at the last minute. Would never miss a golf game, God forbid, even in the winter, but a report on Ms. Day's desk..." She slowly reined in her righteous indignation.

"As I said," and he aimed his most winning smile at her. He liked Janet. He'd had little to do with her among the fifteen hundred people who worked in the White House, at least until these last two weeks. He'd come to appreciate her skills.

She typed a rapid note into her computer—perhaps a log entry on *that Secretary of the Interior.* He knew the man, a pretentious jerk—which Damien felt described a good quarter of the cabinet and at least half of politicians.

"There's a wider world to be appreciated now that I've crawled out of my basement." He'd thought he could see everything, or at least everything important from his watch-duty desk. But up here he'd learned much more about the people who worked to keep the country running than he ever would in his Sit Room.

"Yes, there is," and suddenly Janet's full attention was focused on him.

He had a flash of insight that there just might be someone in this office more dangerous than Cornelia. Her eyes narrowed as she inspected him from head to toe. He was never very comfortable in his dress blues, but at the moment it felt as if he should be wearing them.

"If you are courting Ms. Day, you are doing a poor job of it."

"Courting? What century are you from, Janet?" Personally he thought he was doing a pretty good job of it. They were almost up to their two-week anniversary and she hadn't lost one bit of her shine—Cornelia was still the most fascinating and sexy woman he'd ever been with.

"My Harry courted me from the day we met at the march on Washington to end the Vietnam War in November, 1969. Just because we slept together that first night among the trees by the Reflecting Pool, doesn't mean he didn't still have to win my heart. So don't think you can be all *modern* and dismiss me, young man. A woman likes to be courted, and not only in bed. If you don't get your act together, you're going to lose her. If that happens, I am going to be *very* disappointed in you."

Then she offered one of her matronly smiles.

"You can go in any time you'd like," Janet nodded toward Cornelia's office door before standing to gather her coat and purse.

Damien struggled to his feet and held her coat for her.

After she was gone, Damien sat back down for a moment.

Lose Cornelia? That was not an acceptable scenario.

Did he need to step up his game? That had never been an issue before. He'd also never been so smitten by a woman. No one before Cornelia had engendered thoughts of a permanent nature. Oh, he always had his fantasies of what it might be like to settle down with each woman he met, but it had never felt *important* before. His idle daydreams had been easy to recognize as little more than that.

He studied Janet's vacant desk.

Apparently he wasn't the only one who could imagine a long term scenario between Cornelia and himself. He smacked his forehead with the palm of his hand. He really had to stop thinking like a Marine.

"Are you beating yourself up for any particular reason?"

Cornelia leaned on the door jamb of her office. She actually leaned. Why did such a slight change make her appear so vulnerable? Again his protective, grab-and-hold instincts kicked in.

Tall, elegant in a dark blue outfit that screamed power. Her blouse was a sharp white with a matching mid-waist sash that equally loudly declared feminine. The clothes flowed neatly over her, only appearing to mask the woman within. He knew what lay past the clothes and his first instinct was how much he wanted her body. But he also knew the woman who lived in that incredible body.

"Janet was right," was all he could think to say.

"She usually is," Cornelia agreed. "What about this time?"

"Are you done for the day?" Damien decided that discretion was his best option at the moment. Then he spotted her security badge. His was West Wing-only without an escort—and he'd only rarely had reason to begrudge that, he didn't need more. Hers covered the entire White House. That gave him a great idea.

"Never," her weary smile spoke to the heavy demands of her new job. "But for today, I think so."

"Good! Come along."

"Let me just get my coat."

"You don't need it."

"I'm not going to have sex with you in some White House closet."

"While I like that image a great deal," Janet would kick

his ass, and she'd be right. "I had something else in mind." He rose and held out his elbow, inviting her to take hold, exactly as he had on the walk to Molly Malone's.

After she studied it for a long moment, she stepped forward and did so. The sensation was no different—an essential rightness washed over him as they came in contact. Any man would be proud to escort such a woman anywhere; which didn't do his ego any harm. And maybe it was time to do a little courting.

"I'm not particularly hungry..." her protest died as he turned away from the stairs which led down to the Navy Mess.

———

SOMETHING WAS DIFFERENT ABOUT DAMIEN, AND CORNELIA was too tired to make sense of it. A part of her would be glad to simply go home, let him exhaust her body with his, and hope for some sleep before Saturday morning arrived and the work resumed.

She needed to do something.

Even a quick round of sex in a White House closet didn't sound completely unreasonable at the moment. Something had to happen, because she didn't know how much longer she could hold everything in, and it was only her second week on the job.

Four years loomed impossibly large.

He led her down the hall toward the Oval Office.

No, please, not something *more*.

But he turned aside past the Roosevelt and Cabinet Rooms and along the short hallway to the Western Colonnade.

"I should have taken my coat," she clutched at her

unbuttoned jacket as they stepped outside. The bitter December wind sliced around the tall columns and cut through her poplin blouse.

"Sorry. I didn't want to risk the inside passage through the Press Room to the Residence. Who knows what evil lurks there."

"Reporters," she let a shudder of cold become a mock shudder of horror. "Not tonight. Please."

A Marine in a long pea coat saluted Damien sharply. Damien returned it as neatly and then the Marine, after a glance at her badge, held the Palm Room door for them and she hurried inside—stepping into wonderland.

"It's Christmas," she managed to gasp out. The entry to the Residence was aswirl with decorations. There were trees and such in the West Wing, but nothing like this.

"It is," Damien sounded very smug as he came up beside her.

"As if you are personally responsible."

"Hey! I may not have brought Christmas to you, but I've done a fine job, if I may say so, of bringing you to Christmas."

"It looks to me as if it was already here."

"As if you were going to find time to make it over here on your own. See, personally responsible for taking Ms. Cornelia Day to where Christmas is. That definitely counts."

Cornelia was almost surprised he didn't leap up on a chair and beat his chest to make his point. She could feel herself relaxing. Damien's odd humor always did that to her.

Christmas in Palo Alto, California had never been white, and not even particularly cold. Her family had often traveled up to the city, and San Francisco's damp winters had a penetrating bite to them, but still not snow.

Last week's snowfall had melted away, but the lack of

snow outside the window did nothing to diminish the wonder of Christmas inside the White House as Damien led her into the Central Hall. The decorators had gone mad this year. The low ceiling of the vaulted hallway hadn't made them hesitate for a second. Snowflakes the size of the Capitol Dome were held up by Washington Monument-sized candy canes—or so it seemed. It was overwhelmingly cheerful.

She couldn't wait to see what was upstairs.

But Damien had other ideas and led her deeper into the bowels of the basement. At the midpoint of the long hall, he looked about uncertainly, then led her down a narrow corridor that was crowded to either side with rolled-up rugs and stacked chairs. There was barely room for them to walk side by side.

She glanced at Damien, but he was carefully not meeting her gaze.

"Let's test the power of the White House Chief of Staff," he offered cryptically. The size of his smile was impressive, and very like a little boy's about to be naughty and not caring if he was caught.

They entered another, equally cluttered hall and passed the bowling alley, several storeroom doors, and turned in at the last door down the hall. To the left was a sign for the carpentry shop—she hadn't known that the White House had one of its own. Several offices straight ahead.

To her right a small sign declared: Chocolate Shop.

Damien knocked and the door was opened by a rotund man with a brown-smeared white apron and a tall white hat which had one perfect set of chocolate fingerprints near its base.

"What do ye want?" His brogue was distinctly Scottish.

The chocolatier didn't give them time to answer.

"Never mind, as if I wasn't already knowing. I'm wise to the likes of you." He somehow simultaneously scowled at Damien but winked at her.

He swung the door wider to reveal a fifteen-foot-square stainless steel kitchen packed with refrigerators, supplies, a big stove, and a prep table from which sprouted a four-foot-tall chocolate Christmas tree. The layers of branches were darkest chocolate with milk and white chocolate decorations. Lights were represented by brilliant dots of red, green, and gold fondant.

"You so much as think of touching that and I'll kill you for certain. And if your blood smears a single bit of it, I'll kill myself right here so God help me."

It was a masterpiece and Cornelia wasn't going anywhere near it.

The chef slipped a tray out of a cooler and set it on the counter before them. "Well, don't just look, have at it, won't ye? It's why ye've come nosing about, after all."

Damien grinned at her as he leaned in to inspect the tray.

It was filled with tiny chocolate reindeer. Not flat, like cut out of a sheet of chocolate, but fully three-dimensional figurines, each less than two inches high, including antlers.

"They don't have their harnesses yet, but that's what you get for being the first ones of the season to be comin' by."

They looked charming and delicious.

"Go on, lass. You don't take one and tell me how amazing it is, me heart will be broken fair in two I can promise you."

Cornelia did take one, being very careful not to bump any others. She wasn't quite sure how to eat it.

"Just open up and pop it in."

"I feel like I'm eating Rudolph."

"Nah, I left him and his red nose in the cooler. You're safe with this lot."

Unable to deny his encouraging smile, she did *just pop it in.* And when she bit down it took all her willpower not to spray the Christmas tree with it. The reindeer's body broke apart in her mouth with an unexpected flood of cherry liqueur.

"Oh my God," she managed to mumble as the flavors combined and stormed her senses. "That's incredible."

The chef positively beamed.

———

BY THE TIME THEY ESCAPED, THEY'D EACH HAD A CHERRY reindeer, a peanut butter inside / dark-chocolate outside gnome, and a peppermint snowflake. They'd also shared a tiny glass of schnapps with Chef Andrews—just enough that Damien could feel it warming his blood. As if Cornelia wasn't already doing that.

"Okay, Damien. Top that one," she held onto his arm with both hands and leaned into him as he guided them back into the center of the Residence.

He had no idea how that might be possible. Being strictly West Wing, the chocolate shop had been a rumor he'd only heard about in the past.

Up the stairs to the ground floor, Damien led her through the Entrance Hall, which was more akin to a North Pole snowstorm than a hall, and into the Blue Room. This year's Christmas tree dominated the space, the topmost star nearly brushing the ceiling that normally held the massive gilt-and-crystal French chandelier.

By Cornelia's pleased gasp he knew he'd done well. It

might not be gourmet chocolate, but it was a very pretty tree.

She was completely enamored of it. He'd thought to show it to her and move on to continue their explorations, though he wasn't sure where, but she inspected nearly every ornament.

He read the explanatory placard aloud.

"Immigrant children who came from all over the world to America were invited to paint an ornament like their country of origin's flag. The one hundred and ninety-five countries recognized by the United States are represented here. These include all hundred and ninety-three UN countries as well as the Holy See and Kosovo."

"How many of these have you been to?" Cornelia asked from somewhere farther around the tree.

"Do you see one with a red-and-white maple leaf?"

There was a long pause. "Got it. Canada. Where else?"

"Well, I've been there."

Cornelia looked at him between two branches and an ornament of Trinidad and Tobago's red flag with one black and two white stripes.

"Honest. A Marine cannot tell a lie. I've been to Canada." He held up his right hand with three fingers raised.

"That's the Girl Scout sign," she ducked out of sight as she continued her inspection of the tree.

He looked at his hand. "Actually, I'm fairly sure that's Boy Scouts."

"Girl Scout. Were you ever a Boy Scout?"

"Naw," he lowered his hand, "too busy chasing girls."

"How did that work for you?"

"Sucked. The girls all went for the guys in the cool uniforms."

"That's why you became a Marine?"

"Damn straight."

"I...don't think that I'll ask the next question," she said from somewhere opposite the blue-and-red ornament with a circled red star of North Korea. Must have been a real challenge tracking down a refugee to paint that one. He wondered if the decorators had to make some themselves.

"Well," he couldn't resist the opening, "I'll have to try on my uniform and see what you think."

"I wasn't going to ask," she wandered into sight past the gold, black, and white flag with a red crest that must be Brunei. "Only Canada? Really?"

"Really. I can probably name every flag here because of my time in the Sit Room, but I went from college to officer training, then straight into intel. How about you?"

"I memorized all the flags of the world as a kid. I've been to a lot of countries since Zachary Thomas became Vice President. But I've never seen much of any of them except a monument here and a meeting room there."

How could he not fall for a woman who thought that memorizing all of the flags was something fun to do.

"I try to keep up with the new ones, like Myanmar's change in 2010, but Africa still makes my head hurt. Nothing is stable there for very long."

"Don't feel bad. They make everyone's head hurt. I have a buddy who swears he can tell a map's age within a year out of the last century solely by looking at Africa's changing borders and country names. I have yet to trip him up."

She came up to him until she was so close that he had to put his hands on her waist to keep from stumbling back. "Whoever thought flags could be so sexy?"

Before he could answer, she closed the last of the gap, wrapped her arms around his neck, and kissed him. Janet would be pleased. Hell, *he* was beyond pleased. She kissed him like she meant it.

This wasn't some prelude to sex. It felt like the first time he'd fired a rifle. Handguns he could take or leave, knowledge was his real weapon, but learning to fire an M16A4 had been a voyage of discovery. He never came close to sniper skill. Most of those guys were born with a pop gun in their hands and he'd been born clutching a library card. But a rifle was a machine he'd learned to appreciate. He still tried to get range time every week or so.

Cornelia's kiss was like that. Not sex. Not an unleashing of the passionate woman she normally hid deep inside. It was soft, exploratory, and so sincere that it could take his knees out from under him.

He gave back as good as he could. He rapidly discovered that wasn't a hard task. It was like she was kissing him for the first time and it was a voyage that he wanted to be at the end of as well. The whole ride.

What she seemed to be discovering, he'd already found: exactly who he wanted to be with. And he was holding her.

She—

"I thought that was a Presidential prerogative." Sienna. National Security Advisor. Somewhere behind him.

"What is?" He meant to tell her to go the hell away, but it didn't come out right. He didn't like unanswered questions.

"Necking in the White House."

Oh! "Go away. I'm busy here."

He leaned back in. Cornelia's eyes were dreamy and warm with—

"Have you two eaten yet?"

"What part of *go away I'm busy here* was I unclear about?" But the moment had passed him by. Cornelia's eyes had refocused and were looking over his shoulder toward Sienna.

"No, we haven't eaten."

"Then I'll blame your temporary lapse of protocol on low blood sugar. Come on. Let's go to dinner. You can bring him too if you must."

Cornelia looked at him, "Are you going to behave?"

"Not a chance," his voice was rough and he barely had control.

"I suppose," again she was speaking over his shoulder, "that I'd better bring him along or who knows what trouble he'll get into."

Then she brushed her lips ever so lightly over his.

"This will make us even."

He narrowed his eyes at her.

"Payback," she whispered, "for almost getting me to agree to do it in a White House closet." Cornelia eased away, tucked her hand in his arm, and turned him about. Sienna stood there smirking at them as if she'd heard every word. "He tried to bribe me with chocolate."

And it had damn near worked too. Crap! It had come so close to working, not that getting her naked, in or out of a closet, was his goal at the moment. He needed to get back to finding out what was behind that kiss. He fell into step beside Sienna who slid a hand around his other arm. The two women started talking about something, though he was damned if he could tell what—his ears were still ringing from the stratospheric climb of that kiss.

They headed up some stairs like the three of them were off to see the wizard together. He was in no damn mood to break into a dance step down some yellow brick road.

But maybe he should be. Janet's advice had been spot on. If this was the result of doing a little courting, he was going to try it again soon. Hell, he'd do it every damn day for the rest of his life.

Cornelia had kissed him with more than her body, she'd done it with her heart. Did she even realize that?

He'd bet not and it was going to surprise the crap out of her when she did. He couldn't wait to be the one to tell her. He almost *did* want to break into a dance as they turned along a hall.

He'd dance right down the yellow...Oval Room.

The Yellow Oval was on the floor directly above the Blue Room with its Christmas tree.

That placed the Yellow Oval on the second floor, the President's personal residence.

He swallowed hard and blinked a few times. It didn't go away. He'd stumbled to a halt. Clicking his heels three times didn't make it go away.

For the first time in a decade at the White House, he was in the President's home.

———

"Look what I found wandering the halls," Sienna called out to the assembled group.

Cornelia welcomed the abrupt change of scene.

Here the world made more sense than in the highly decorated first floor and Blue Room. Anywhere in the world made more sense than the Blue Room at the moment.

Each year at Christmas she had been invited, along with Vice President Thomas, to the President's Christmas party. And though the night of the formal party was still a week away, it was a familiar sight.

The Central Hall of the Second Floor of the Residence had far more rational seasonal decorations than the floors below. There were a couple of cheerful Christmas trees glittering in the long space. Red poinsettias ringed the grand piano. Festive pine-and-citrus garlands had been draped about dour eighteenth-century paintings. And that was about the extent of it—cheery without overwhelming.

In among the décor, President Peter Matthews, Zachary, Daniel, and a man she didn't know had gathered on a group of couches. Then Sienna wrapped an arm about the stranger's neck and leaned down to kiss him. This had to be Roy Beaumont, Sienna's Secret Service sniper fiancé. The men all looked casually comfortable together. She wondered if she was really supposed to be here, then remembered that she was the Chief of Staff now—not merely the Vice President's assistant.

She didn't normally gravitate to groups, but at the moment she greeted them and tried to hurry along the lagging Damien next to her.

The kiss in the Blue Room hadn't been merely intense. Damien was the master of intense, which worked for her because so was she. But that kiss had been...languid. Not that there wasn't energy, but rather that there was a smooth perfection that had filled her body until she felt as if she was radiating light out of every pore.

Cornelia Day the Christmas ornament.

It was the only way that she could describe it. Deep and smooth, it had flowed through and out of her. Rather than leaving her breathless for more, it had grounded her with a completeness that...

That she'd never found anywhere before. Sex with Damien was great. Actually, spectacular. But it was still sex. The kiss was something different that she really wasn't ready to think about.

"Since when..." Zachary was eyeing their still-clasped hands.

When Cornelia attempted to extract hers from Damien's, he resisted. She finally accepted the inevitable and ceased her effort. It was too late to hide anyway.

"Need to pay closer attention, Mr. President-elect," Daniel teased Zachary. "They're an item. Hot gossip for days now."

"A week," President Matthews put in.

"You're all blind," Sienna stood beside her fiancé's chair with a hand on his shoulder. "They've been together since the first day in the Sit Room. Totally obvious. Though I think Cornelia was a little slow on the uptake on that."

"Never known her to be slow about anything." Zachary was studying her more closely than she was comfortable with. She had always kept her personal life separate from the office, never mentioning a boyfriend, always being careful to cancel a date out of earshot if there was a late change in work plans.

Damien nodded agreement that Sienna had it right and the other men inspected him with renewed interest. She could see that slightly smug aura of self-satisfaction coming from him. *I'm the new alpha male on the block* simply radiated in every direction. She could even feel it in the strengthening of his grip on her hand.

Before she could do anything to knock him back to reality, Sienna stepped over and extracted Cornelia's hand from Damien's. Then she shoved Damien toward one of the vacant chairs.

"Come on," Sienna kept Cornelia's hand in hers and led her back toward the stair landing, through a grand arched passage, and into the East Sitting Hall. It was tucked between the Lincoln Bedroom and the Queen's Bedroom.

First Lady Kim-Ly Geneviève *Genny* Matthews had decorated the space for herself with an eclectic mix of her combined French-Vietnamese heritage. Comfortable chairs, intricately carved side tables, wall pieces in dark wood, and pots of lush plants leant a tamed-jungle feel to the space.

It was as breathtaking as the woman with a thick flow of dark brown hair who sat with the First Child asleep in her lap.

Daniel's wife and CIA analyst Alice Darlington, and First Lady-elect Anne Darlington-Thomas completed the small group.

She definitely did *not* belong here. Men she knew how to deal with, even Damien's ego, but these women were a mystery, even if she *had* become close friends with Anne—at least close enough that she'd stood maid-of-honor for her. But her life had been so busy in the months since that even that felt tenuous at best.

Sienna dragged her along by the hand that she hadn't released since freeing it from Damien's clasp—as if she'd known Cornelia's reaction ahead of time. She led them to an open couch and pulled Cornelia down beside her.

"I caught her and Damien Feinman necking by the Blue Room Christmas tree. I figured I'd better drag her to safety, because it looked like one of *those* kisses."

All eyes turned on her.

"Really?" Anne's question was filled with hope as she leaned forward to pour two glasses of wine for the late arrivals. "I do so *love* those kinds of kisses."

Alice and the First Lady were nodding in agreement as Sienna sighed happily at some memory of her own.

If this was safety, Cornelia was going to go back to California and study to be a dentist.

"So, you and my Chief of Staff?" Zachary Thomas asked as Damien returned from the family kitchen with a beer for himself and a refresher for Roy and the President.

"Seems like," Damien tried not to sound too damn pleased, but it was hard.

"Who's first?" The President asked the others.

"Who's first what?"

Everyone else appeared to know what he was talking about.

"They're debating," Daniel explained with a sweep of his beer glass to indicate the others, "which one will get first shot at beating the stuffing out of you if you hurt her in any way."

"Oh," Damien suddenly felt much less comfortable. This circle was several leagues above his usual social set.

"The Commander in Chief," Daniel continued amiably, "is partial to the Night Stalkers helicopter regiment. I know from personal experience that having them on your bad side is not a good choice. Though I'm not sure having them on your good side is all that much better. They're a tough crowd."

"As a Secret Service sniper turned Protection Detail," Roy spoke up, "I'll just shoot your ass and be done with you."

"Like the President," Zachary Thomas picked up without missing a beat, "I'm partial to helicopters. But I flew combat search-and-rescue for the Air Force. So, I'll be obliged to save your ass after the Night Stalkers dump you in the middle of the Hindu Kush without two sticks to rub together and Roy then shoots your ass for you. Of course, in another seven weeks I'll also have the authority to call up a flight of A-10 Warthogs or a couple B-2 stealth bombers to take you out immediately afterward."

"So don't screw up, because we aren't the dangerous ones," Daniel concluded.

Damien blew out a hard breath. "Well if you guys aren't, then who is?"

In unison all the guys turned to face toward the latest round of women's laughter sounding from down the hall where Cornelia had gone.

"Okay," he couldn't argue with that.

The President nodded, as if confirming that topic was laid to rest.

"So, where's the money on tomorrow's game?" Zachary spoke up. "My Air Force Falcons have already won Commander in Chief's Trophy by lambasting both the Army and the Navy."

Damien groaned, "One lousy point. The Falcons beat the Academy's Midshipmen by one lousy point. That's not a lambasting."

"Still a win for the Air Force," Zachary sat back with all the arrogance of a President-elect whose school had the winning team.

"We're going to trounce the Army," Damien declared.

"You're only safe saying that because there isn't anyone from the Army here to defend their school."

"We'll trounce them anyway."

"Should I call up Majors Beale and Henderson and ask their opinion?" The President's question was an outright dare.

Damien had met the Majors. Even retired and working as aviation firefighters, he wasn't going to tangle with them.

"We're still gonna win," he tried not to be sullen about how poor their starting lineup was this year.

The others laughed in commiseration.

————

"SERIOUSLY! WE NEED TO GO DOWN AND RAID THAT chocolate shop now," Sienna was immediately on her feet at the end of Cornelia's telling the tale.

"It will spoil our appetites," Anne pointed out. "Dinner is soon."

"Nonsense. Chocolate has nothing to do with appetite spoilage," Alice rose to clasp an arm around Sienna's shoulders. "We're starting a women-in-search-of-chocolate solidarity movement. Who's on board?"

Cornelia was on the verge of caving to the inevitable when the First Lady spoke softly.

"Adele is still asleep," she nodded toward the two-year old half on the couch and half in her mother's lap. "But I have a solution. Could you hand me the phone?"

Cornelia did so while the two women in solidarity looked on.

"Chef Andrews? Genny Matthews here up in East Sitting Hall. Cornelia Day has been regaling us with the wonders of your confections and we were hoping that we might send someone down to fetch a sampling... Oh. Perfect! Thank you." She hung up the phone. "He is sending it right up. Apparently he had been experimenting with the Marou chocolate that I brought him from my last trip to Vietnam and would appreciate some *biased* opinions. We should be in for a treat."

There was an effortlessness to the First Lady that Cornelia wished she possessed.

"You are inspecting me with deep thoughts."

Somewhat abashed, Cornelia repeated her thought aloud.

"Yes, it is just so. That is how I may appear, but I did not feel this way when your President was proposing to me while a renegade faction of the Thai army was attacking us in Cambodia."

"Damien hasn't proposed to me."

"And yet," Genny said with her perfect calm, "he is the first thought when you think of proposals. The first time Peter and I played Scrabble, that is when I knew, though I could not accept it until my grandmother told me it was a truth. We played where the men are sitting even now. It was our third meeting."

Cornelia opened her mouth and closed it again.

"There are times when you simply know," Anne reassured her. "I was done in by a photograph of a model train set."

"Daniel being outsmarted by an Advent Calendar," Alice sighed.

"When Roy aimed his rifle at me," Sienna shrugged at Cornelia's surprise. "I should say his rifle scope, but the two pieces were attached at the time. He simply couldn't stop watching me. Still can't."

"He is the head of your protection detail," Anne pointed out.

"Yes, though he still enjoys filling in on the roof sniper overwatch when I'm not traveling—even in this weather."

Cornelia shuddered all the way down to her California upbringing.

"Besides, I prefer to think it is my magnetic powers. Though I have to admit, the moment I met him face-to-face —*phfftt!*" She flicked aside the fall of hair by her temple. "Instant brain short. Other than insulting him a few times at the Air and Space Museum, I can't remember a thing I said to him. I suppose that I should have known then, but it took me longer than these others."

"Well, we had our first kiss in front of the Air and Space Museum." Cornelia could remember every moment of that kiss, so why was the one in the Blue Room little more than a hazy blur yet ten times more important?

"Yum," Sienna agreed. "Great spot."

"Except it was dark, cold, and snowing."

"All the more reason to grab a warm man."

Had that been her moment?

Perhaps during that first meeting across the Sit Room table where she discovered an intelligence to match her own? Or at his look of interest across that table when he had discovered the same?

No. That had been interest. It had been...

"For our first date—I didn't even know that's what it was —he took me to Molly Malone's. It's an Irish pub across the street from the Marine Barracks. It was a Friday night and the restaurant was packed with very able-bodied men."

The others *oohed* and *aahed*.

"*Very* able bodied," Cornelia wasn't exactly sure what came over her—she'd barely noticed the other men—but her tease was met with more groans of delight. "Yet he was so sure of himself that he never for a moment second-guessed taking me there. At least not until I pointed out his potential folly." And they all laughed.

And Cornelia *knew*.

Exactly as the other women had known.

That had been the moment that Damien swept her off her feet—almost literally when his friend had pounded him on the back. It was his confidence, yes. But most of all it was his easy willingness to laugh at himself first of anyone. Here was a man who sat in the one place in the world best suited to see mankind's worst moments—disaster had a direct feed to his desk—yet still found paths to joy.

"Aren't they the cutest thing when they're so sure of themselves?" Sienna sighed happily.

They were, Cornelia agreed, but it wasn't without reason.

Any further discussion was interrupted by the arrival of Chef Andrews himself. He'd changed to a clean apron, though he'd missed the chocolate fingerprints on his chef's hat as he delivered a whole new range of chocolate delicacies for them to sample.

11

"WHAT IS GOING ON WITH YOU?"

Damien did his best to look innocent at Cornelia's question.

It had been another week since their *Residence Date* as they were calling it between them—their impromptu dinner with the First Family both present and future.

A week filled with frustration as everyone weighed in on the possible meanings of President Madani's warning. Suggestions, which had flowed in so thick and fast in the beginning, were petering out due to lack of even the slimmest supporting evidence. Analysts were scrabbling through signal data with equally little luck. There was simply *none* of the typical signs of a pending attack.

Many now thought that it was a false alarm.

But none of them had sat with Cornelia Day in Katz's and heard the Madani's assured tone.

"All week you've been far more...solicitous."

Without Janet's suggestion, he'd never have thought to take Cornelia to the West Wing to see Christmas or stumbled into that wonderful dinner. He'd learned a powerful lesson from that.

Tonight, when Cornelia was too busy to take a break, he'd gone out into the dark night and picked up some take-out Chinese. They were presently eating at the big oak conference table in her office, while eager little porcelain reindeer watched them carefully. She flipped through a thick file as she ate. Janet had declined to join them as her husband was arriving soon to take her out to dinner.

She used her chopsticks neatly to pick up a slice of lemon chicken as she continued flipping through the file.

"Was I that bad before?" If so, he didn't want to hear about it.

"No, you were wonderful before. Now you've tipped over into amazing." Cornelia continued doing three things at once as neatly as she always did everything.

In fact, the only time he'd ever seen her do only one thing at a time was when she was in his arms—which he decided he should take as a high compliment.

"So, what are you up to, Feinman?"

Janet came in with a stack of memos. Most, he was glad to see, were only one or two pages long. Out of sight of Cornelia, she sent him a broad wink.

"Well," he kept a weather eye on Janet so that he could gauge her reaction. "Being solicitous is what comes from being in love with you."

Janet's snort of laughter wasn't seemly on a woman of her age and dignity.

That dragged Cornelia's full attention out of her file, even making her chopsticks pause halfway back to her bowl. She looked at Janet, who wasn't making the least attempt to appear innocent, then at him.

"You," she pointed her chopsticks at Janet, "have been messing with my dating life. What did you do to Damien?"

"Oh no, Ms. Day. I would never do that," shocked hand to ruffled blouse.

"You should have been an actress," Damien should never have said a thing to begin with. It only encouraged them.

"I might interfere with your *love life* though. Your boy needed a good nudge."

"Hey. I'm a man, not a boy. And that wasn't a nudge, it was more like a hard boot in the ass."

"Shush when your elders are speaking."

"She threatened me," he did his best to make it sound like he was a whining child. It didn't help that she was right.

"Threatened you about what?"

Damien caved, "Taking you to the West Wing to see Christmas was only partly my idea. She," Damien pointed an accusing finger, "said I should be paying more attention to you the person than you—" he almost said *the goddess in my bed* but caught himself in time, "—as a girlfriend."

Janet's glare told him he was entering the danger zone. Maybe he *should* listen to himself and keep his mouth shut.

"Would have helped if she hadn't been so right," he grumbled out the last, ignoring his own directive.

"He's a good sort, Ms. Day, best I've seen since my Harry. Damien merely required a little hint to bring out the best in him."

Damien kept his *harrumph* to himself.

"Now what has Cornelia Day in such a twist?" Janet actually planted her fists on her hips like some over-dramatic actress.

"I'm not in a twist," she denied Janet's accusation. "Except over the latest disaster that is Egyptian politics,"

Cornelia tapped a finger on the thick file she'd been studying.

"But—" Then Damien bit down on his tongue remembering his own *be silent* advice.

Janet was looking at him. Waiting.

"But you are." She was. "And have been since the dinner in the Residence last week."

Janet nodded as if once again he'd done something right. "Don't stop there, young man." She set the memos on Cornelia's desk and headed back to her own.

"What's going on, Cornelia?" He kept his voice low. Not because he was trying to hide anything from Janet; that was clearly a waste of time. Rather he did it to soothe whatever was bothering her.

"What do you mean?" She stabbed her chopsticks hard into a perfectly innocent piece of shrimp egg foo yung and left them there.

"Ever since that night you've been even more yourself than usual. More studiously Cornelia Day than the Cornelia Day I met in the Sit Room that first day."

"You're making as much sense as usual," she reached for her file, but he intercepted her hand and trapped it between his. He could feel nerves coursing within her that he hadn't noticed until this moment.

"You are brilliantly meticulous. You are my idol of rational thought. Just to be clear, I'm not accusing you of being Spock."

"That's good," her voice went suddenly small and he realized how many men must have said that or something similar to her. Only someone who didn't know her would call her *ice bitch* but he could practically hear the phrase echoing about her. So many times that she had come to believe it of herself. She gave a chilly first impression when she was in her work mode.

"It's not true. All those assholes were wrong. You have more warmth and passion inside you than any woman I've ever met."

"You haven't met many women then."

"Like you? I've met a grand total of one, Cornelia. You're it. That's why I can say I love you and mean it. Nobody gobsmacks me the way you do."

She looked up at him and impossibly she looked to be on the verge of tears. He wasn't sure he could handle a crying Cornelia Day. His world wasn't structured for such things.

"But all week you've been ever so careful. Last week you were slouching against a door jamb while Janet teased me and looking relaxed about the whole situation between us. I haven't seen you out of your formal best since." He indicated her buttoned blazer. "What's going on, my lady?"

"My lady? Now you're getting all knightly on me?"

"Hello, Marine and librarian. I come by noble and knightly and arcane—all three—completely naturally. What do you do completely naturally?"

"Being a stone cold bitch," it came out on a gasp of pain that totally belied the words.

Shit! He hated that he was right.

"Well, either I'm attracted to stone cold bitches, or everyone in your past was an idiot."

"Which seems more likely?"

"That they were all idiots. Seriously, you're lucky you found me. New evidence, fresh in, shows that most of my gender are utter goons."

Cornelia sniffled and looked at him, really looked at him.

He didn't carry a handkerchief. He'd always thought it too old-fashioned but now he wished he had one. He'd buy a whole stack tomorrow. In the meantime he lightly brushed a knuckle past the corners of her eyes and it came away wet.

"You really do love me."

She didn't make it a question, but he nodded to confirm the truth—as much inside himself as for her. It really wasn't a question.

"That's what happened to me last week in the Residence, before the dinner," her voice was a gentle whisper.

"What?"

She touched the ends of her chopsticks but didn't retrieve them from the heart of the egg foo young. "I understood that I loved you."

The soft words didn't slam into him as he'd expected. Instead they were a gentle wash over him, a benediction as solid and complete as his oath of office on the day he became a Marine Corps officer.

When he leaned in to kiss her, she tasted of soy sauce and salty tears.

Then she silently rose, indicating he should stay seated. She stepped over to her office door, looked briefly into the darkened outer office, then closed and locked it. Turning off the lights, she crossed back to him.

The lights of the EEOB filtered through the curtains and the dark winter's night as she sat straddling his lap.

"It's not a closet, but I hope it will do," she whispered as she embraced him.

This time all he could taste on her lips was her smile.

———

MAKING LOVE TO DAMIEN IN HER OWN OFFICE FELT RISQUÉ, wild even. Cornelia decided that maybe she needed that in her life. Maybe the cold that she thought wrapped around her came as much from the inside as the outside.

As his lips traced down her neck, she leaned her elbows back on the conference table, opening herself to him. He unbuttoned her blouse and, as he continued his journey, she ran her hands through his soft hair.

Maybe she had become the job *too* completely. It was necessary. Zachary Thomas was overly charitable with his time. He was a good man who needed someone to control how much came to his attention and how quickly.

She had become his control until she embodied it.

As Damien eased her bra aside, some part of that control slipped away. A piece of that hard shell broke off and scattered like snow onto the white carpet. And when he lay her there, naked beneath him, warm and safe in his arms, her shields shattered.

The ever-so-studiously constructed Cornelia Day that she had first formed as a precocious, over-tall preteen had become more than a persona—it had become her.

Yet Damien had seen past that from the first moment. And he proved once more, evoking responses she'd never known were possible, that he would never see her any other way. Not merely desirable, which would have been a big enough surprise on its own, but as worthy in and of herself.

She'd always presented that to the world.

But as Damien made love to her, she knew all the way to her core that she truly was worthy of a man like him.

12

"A TUBA CHRISTMAS?"

"Tonight at the Library of Congress. Led by the Marine Corps Band tuba section."

Cornelia stared at Damien. "You do understand what's happening here?" They sat alone in the Sit Room.

He waved a hand at the massive files spread between them. "I've been reading the same things you have. What's happening is absolutely *nothing*. Every single idea here is conjecture. Whatever President Javad Madani heard, there isn't a shred of evidence that any of our intelligence agencies can scare up."

"But—" He cut her off with a raised hand.

"I'm not saying that his warning isn't valid. I'm saying that we don't have a single hypothesis or communication here that gives us the least insight into its meaning. This—" he gestured helplessly at the pile of reports perfectly mirroring his own feelings, "—mess isn't helping us with anything."

She knew that. The problem was that as their *Christian holiday season* was fast coming to a close, the number of days in which an attack was possible were decreasing. Most leaders of intelligence and Homeland Security now agreed that it was a non-event.

Even if President Madani had heard a valid rumor, they still insisted, *that doesn't mean it actually came together.*

"The naysayers' perspective is *not* invalid." Cornelia pointed out. "No chatter. No unusual activity."

"We're the last true believers," Damien sighed and looked back down at the files.

That was what had drawn them together, to double-team the files once more in the hopes of finding some overlooked connection. Six hours later all it had earned them was a frustration that almost had them sniping at each other.

We shall cut out their heart with their own words.

"No unusual activity near the inscriptions on the Lincoln Memorial," Damien shoved aside one report. "No unusual activity at the Supreme Court or the Library of Congress. Scans of surveillance footage at the Capitol record only the usual crazies. It's even been too damn cold for all but the most hard core protestors on the Mall." Report after report was shoved aside until the only thing remaining was the slim file of her initial debriefing.

Damien flipped it open and began reading Madani's words aloud:

What can be done to help the gulf between us?

When in the course of human events it becomes necessary for people of good will to come together over good food.

This time the storm enters from the Bay, not the Gulf.

President Matthews had explained that one. President Madani had helped him foil a bio-weapon of mass destruction from being smuggled in through the Gulf of

Mexico. So, not the *Gulf* this time. The Chesapeake Bay still remained their most likely candidate.

An attack coming. It is neither chemical nor biological. I am informed that it is cultural.

We shall cut out their heart with their own words.

I can only offer you my prayers during this, your Christian holiday season.

Cornelia sighed. She'd read every one of those phrases a hundred times until they were ingrained in her memory.

A very discreet inquiry through the US interests section of the Swiss embassy in Tehran—technically the only diplomatic connection between the two countries—had returned two words from Pejman: *Nothing further.*

"I wish we could call Javad right now and ask again."

"You wouldn't be able to reach him tonight."

"Why not?"

Damien flicked on the microphone that would connect the watch desk and said aloud, "*Shab-e Yalda.* We'll see how long it takes them to figure that one out."

Within moments a watermelon and a pomegranate appeared on the screens.

"Not very long, I guess," Cornelia looked at them. "What do they have in common other than both being red and messy to eat?"

As if in answer, a title appeared on the other screen.

Shab-e Yalda: Winter Solstice Party (Iran)

Successive lines were typed in rapidly:

Highly popular gatherings where food, drink, and poetry (esp. by Hafez) are shared

Typically lasts past midnight

Red fruit symbolizes dawn and life

Gatherings symbolize coming together in times of darkness

"All right, already. Enough," Damien called out.

One more line appeared before they stopped:

Ancient origin: Celebrates triumph of Mithra—Sun God— over darkness

"You done good, Bettani."

"Suck my tush, Damien," a woman managed over her own laughter.

It was the first time Cornelia had ever heard any at the watch desk talk back, or talk at all to the Sit Room. She liked that they felt comfortable enough to do it, even knowing she was there as well as Damien.

"As I said, big party." Then he made a loud raspberry sound before flicking off the mic switch. "So, I have a suggestion."

"A tuba Christmas?"

"Absolutely."

Cornelia looked at the pile covering half of the big conference table and decided that maybe he was right.

———

THE STREETS WERE TOO BITTERLY COLD TO WALK. Washington often dropped below freezing, but fifteen degrees was frosty even by a Marine's standards. They caught the Metrorail to Capitol South and nearly froze as they hustled the two blocks through the dusk and Friday evening traffic that was always completely mad around the Capitol Building itself.

"I can't believe you've never been to the Library of Congress. How in the world can I be in love with a woman who has never been there?"

"I don't have a lot of time to read. Especially lately," Cornelia pulled her scarf tighter and hurried faster along the icy sidewalk. Damn but the woman had legs, he practically had to jog to keep up with her long stride.

He risked a laugh and nearly froze his lungs.

"If this is an outdoor concert, you're a dead man."

"It's not. Besides, the Library of Congress isn't only about books to read."

"What else then?"

"I'll show you," he decided that stopping to admire the Court of Neptune Fountain and its stunning bronze statuary would probably get him attacked.

"Right, like a tuba Christmas." He ignored her sarcasm and led her up the broad flight of stone stairs.

"I've always loved the Library of Congress; this is what a library should look like." The Thomas Jefferson Building covered an entire city block and rose three full stories. The main steps led them into the middle story. The Ground Floor was all offices and archives. The entry was at the first story.

Not pausing at the main arches—it was really too cold to stop and point out the busts of history's great writers stationed in circular windows far above—they practically burst through the front doors into the Great Hall.

Cornelia staggered to a stop and looked about in clear shock. It was one of the grandest rooms in all of DC architecture and yet almost nobody came here. The palatial hall soared aloft for two towering stories. Grand, white marble staircases swept up either side of the hall, ornate with deeply carved balustrades. The upper story was all arches and columns making the area feel even larger because it appeared to have no bounds. And in the center stood a grand Christmas tree that looked utterly impossible in the space.

"How?" Cornelia whispered in a gasp of shock. "How did they get that tree in here? It's so perfect."

"It's a secret. I could tell you, except you're not a librarian."

In moments she'd inspected the roof, the entryways, even tapped a foot on the dark marble of the inlaid floor.

"They use a magic wand."

She rolled her eyes at him and moved closer to the tree. Over a dozen feet at the base, it towered over twenty feet high in a near perfect cone. Its branches were thick with ornaments—They were books! Or book *covers* at least. Afloat in a sea of sparkling lights.

"Every librarian was asked for their two favorite books: one of historical significance, one of modern enjoyment. The top two hundred titles were painted up as ornaments: a hundred historic, a hundred modern."

"That explains the crazy collection of titles. Which were your two?" She began moving around the tree reading as she went. He followed, not wanting to be left behind again. There were perhaps fifty people already gathered for the concert, it was early yet. But several were walking about the tree, making shouting through it awkward.

"I'm not an LOC librarian so I didn't get a vote. But if I had to choose, I'd say *Beowulf* as the first work in English Literature."

"Which you have, of course, read in the original."

"I took it as a challenge in high school. Ended up doing my own translation, which was fairly crappy, but I did it. And I've always been a John le Carré fan. The old spy thrillers. How about you?"

"You probably tried passing girls mash notes in old English."

"Might have. And they might have been in alliterative verse as well," he admitted. "There he is," he spotted the *Beowulf* cover. "So I'm not the only arcane one in the building."

"And I'm sure those poems helped you be even more popular with the teenage girls attracted to Boy Scouts in uniform."

"Not particularly," he grimaced. Nothing quite cut to the core like a teenage girl's laugh of amused dismissal.

"I'd choose *Anne of Green Gables* or *Secret Garden* for the historical," she pointed to both of them, then tipped her head as she gazed up at the tree either thinking or reading titles. "For the modern day, I think I'd have to say *Landmarks* by Robert Macfarlane."

"I...don't know that one."

"It's about language, especially geographic language, and how it works."

He thumped a hand over his heart. He'd fallen for a woman who thought linguistics was worth reading about for the sake of itself.

"I'll get it for you for Christmas."

That one stopped him cold. Granted it was only four days away, but it was the very first time either of them had spoken of any plans further away than the next meal. It was going to be their first Christmas together.

"What?" Cornelia was inspecting him with those dark eyes he could get so completely lost in. *Could get? That ship already left the harbor, Damien.*

"Christmas. Together."

She shrugged, "I'll probably have to work."

"Doesn't matter. As long as I get to spend it with you."

She did that head-tip thing that he'd so come to enjoy. "You *are* a romantic."

"You're only now figuring that out?"

"I'll bet you want a tree."

"I bet that I already have one at my apartment."

She turned from the huge pine to eye him carefully, "Does it already have a wrapped present under it, in case you could 'wrangle' me there?"

"It might," he shouldn't have admitted even that. What if she was irritated? Or put off? Or—

She stepped into his arms and kissed him—in the Library of Congress.

Life simply didn't get any better.

"What am I going to do with you? No, wait. Don't answer that. That was the wrong question to ask a romantic so close before Christmas."

"It was," he admitted. He knew exactly what he hoped to do with her, both in short- and long-term scenarios.

———

Cornelia definitely wasn't ready for this. She had fallen in love with a romantic who was already thinking of marriage. "That gift under your tree had better not be a goddamn ring," she whispered to him.

"Not an idiot. I'm not going to propose in our first month together," Then that I'm-about-to-be-really-charming smile of his broke out. "I'm going to wait until at least New Years."

She fisted him lightly in the gut.

He spotted it in time, so her fist merely bounced off his hard abs.

"Where are the tubas you wanted to show me?" Because she certainly needed a distraction from whatever else was going on here.

"A tuba Christmas is something you hear, not see."

"You're talking about actual tubas doing what, playing Christmas carols?"

"Exactly. But they don't start for a bit. Let's take the ten-cent tour."

She had never once planned a date as thoroughly as Damien planned every little outing. He was slippery and she was going to have to watch him like a hawk over the years to come.

Years to come. *Right. Because they'd be working together in the White House together.* Though she knew that wasn't what she'd meant. They had been discussing wedding rings only seconds ago.

Well, Cornelia, how far astray can a man lead you in a library?

She waved for him to begin the tour.

And he did. Either he'd studied for their date on the off chance that she'd agree to it, or he knew the building as well as any guide. Classic paintings of justice, corruption, balance, and bad legislation.

From the Visitor's Gallery on the second floor, she could look down on the Main Reading Room exactly as it had appeared in a hundred movies: three great circles of reading desks around an inner circle of the librarian's desk. What the movies never seemed to capture was the magnificent dome above.

"The eight muses in marble," Damien pointed them out high on the dome's structure where the great arches came together. "Art, Science, Religion—all women."

"As they should be," she teased him.

"But the paired bronzes below them, each pair representing the muse above them, are all men: Michelangelo and Beethoven for art, Christopher

Columbus and Robert Fulton for Commerce, and so on. See? It's proof that men are good at getting things done."

"Sure, after the women think them up."

"Behind every successful man is a good woman."

"Because he needs one," but Cornelia couldn't help glancing over her shoulder. So who stood behind *her*?

Who stood behind a successful woman, especially if she had missed something crucial and Javad Madani's warning *was* real?

Who would stand beside her and help her be strong if hundreds or even thousands died because of something *she* had missed?

"Don't worry, babe," Damien slipped a hand around her waist. "I've got your back."

Would he if he knew what he'd signed up for? That almost made her laugh. But it would be a sad, morose sound, so she kept it inside. If anyone knew what they'd signed up for on this one, it would be the Situation Room librarian.

"Oh, there's something else you have to see," and Damien was tugging on her hand as he led her deeper into the building.

In an exhibition hall, a dozen documents were set out in formidable glass cases.

"This is the first map on which the word 'America' appears, 1507. This is our birth certificate in a way, fifteen years after Columbus." The new continents were long, thin things ranging north and south with a gap between the continents at the Isthmus of Panama, a gap that would take over four hundred more years to create. But there, just below the drawing of a parrot was the word *America*.

Right next to it was...

"The rough draft of the Declaration of Independence. How cool is that?"

Cornelia would have to admit, it was pretty cool.

"When in the course of human events it becomes necessary..." she read aloud and felt a chill run up her spine.

"Okay, a little creepy under the circumstances, but look at what Franklin and Adams did to it. Talk about tough editors." The four-page manuscript had dozens of cross-outs and corrections, all done in flowing pen-and-ink script. No tracked changes on a computer document with annotations asking additional questions to accept or reject. These were strong, definitive edits that had created a nation two-and-a-half two centuries before.

Damien was like a boy in a candy store with a twenty-dollar bill. There was too much to show her, too many options. The next room was a circle in a square. It was a high, square room with all of the architectural ornamentation displayed elsewhere in the building, but set upon the intricate blue-and-white marble floor stood a circle of tall, glassed-in bookcases. At this hour they were the room's sole occupants; everyone else who arrived this late in the evening was here for the Christmas concert.

"Jefferson's personal library," Damien declared proudly as if he'd installed it himself. "He sold it to the country after the British burned the first library along with the White House and the Capitol back in 1814. He kept the books in a circle because he wanted to be at the center of knowledge."

Cornelia slowly turned to study the thousands of volumes arrayed there.

"And they weren't organized by author or size like most prior libraries. He broke them into forty-four chapters of knowledge grouped under three major headings: Memory, Reason, and Imagination. I would give anything to have been able to sit with him for even an hour and talk about his classification system alone."

Damien's passion was overwhelming.

"Why don't you work here?"

"At the LOC? Too quiet. That's the Marine in me. Once I became hooked on intel and current affairs, I couldn't turn back. Maybe some day, after they kick me out for slovenly behavior or some crime against protocol like hitting on the White House Chief of Staff, I'll come work here. Over a hundred-and-sixty million items in the collection; it's the largest library in the world. Did you know that they have every tweet from Twitter filed a hundred feet down this hallway?"

"The center of knowledge..."

"Absolutely," he tugged her arm until they were in the exact center of the rosette on the floor. "Can't you just feel it."

"When in the course of human events..."

"Wait, what?" Damien turned to her.

"*We shall cut out their heart with their own words.* That's what Pejman said their source said."

Cornelia tried not to be sick in the middle of Thomas Jefferson's library. She clutched onto his shoulder for support.

"Damien. We're standing in the center of knowledge as far as the United States of America is concerned. We're in a building bursting at the seams with our own words. And we're not a hundred feet from the first draft of the Declaration of Independence."

———

Damien's vision blurred with the shock. He'd heard the phrase before, but never given it any credence—until this moment.

Then his vision, literally, went red. Someone was setting out to destroy the Library of Congress. They were going to destroy a library. This one! Grander than the ancient Library of Alexandria.

"When? When do you think it will happen?" Cornelia's brain was still working.

All he cared about at the moment was murdering somebody with his bare hands. He dragged himself back from the edge, forcing his own thoughts into motion.

"Before our *Christian holiday season is over.* Maybe we have some time?"

Damien looked at the beautiful collection around him. A part of him wanted to own every one of these books so that he too could someday sit at the center of knowledge as Jefferson had. No, he wanted to rush the collection out of the building right now so that they'd be safe.

And then he knew.

"No, we don't have time."

"Why not?"

"The last line of Bettani's report." He was going to have to kiss her for putting that last line up on the screen—if he lived that long.

"Shab-e Yalda. *Celebrates triumph of Mithra—Sun God— over darkness.*"

She offered him her first-ever laugh in his presence, but it was a harsh and bitter sound that echoed strangely from the glassed-in circle of bookcases. "I guess you're not the only one with an arcane sense of humor."

"Tonight. It's the solstice. This is Mithra's battle of the

light of Islam extremists over the darkness of the United States of America."

Cornelia yanked out her phone, studied the contacts list for a moment, then hit dial.

Damien did the same. He had the NSA on speed dial.

"This is Damien Feinman. We've been chasing the wrong keywords on this warning from Iran. Check for chatter on Shab-e Yalda." Unlike Bettani, he had to spell it for them.

He'd have to remember to tell Bettani that too if he ever saw her again.

———

"Ms. Day. How nice of you to call at eight o'clock on a Friday night," General Arnson's tone was friendly, but dry as week-old toast.

What was it with self-confident men and their need to tease women? She didn't have time to puzzle at it right now and it was probably a simple reality that was pointless to file away for future consideration.

"What can I do for you?"

"I'm not sure who to call, but I think we have trouble."

"You solved President Madani's puzzle?" She suddenly had his full attention.

"We think so. The Library of Congress, tonight, and I didn't know who better to call."

"It just so happens that you called exactly the right person, my daughter and future son-in-law are here for dinner." Then he shouted in the background, "Sienna. Target is Library of Congress, tonight. Get to the White House and roust the President. Roy, wake up those lazy dogs you work with at the Secret Service."

"Damien is already in contact with the NSA, not your daughter the National Security Advisor, but rather the National Security Agency," Cornelia wasn't sure why she felt the sudden need to explain the obvious. Perhaps because it was the only way to make sense of what was happening at the moment.

It was her first inkling that she was afraid. She forced her voice to remain steady.

"They're checking for chatter on a new set of keywords."

Even as she said it she saw Damien close his eyes and tip his head back in frustration. "Check for frequency versus prior years. It *is* an annual holiday," he groaned into his phone.

"It looks like we have a confirmation on tonight, but he's still checking."

"Well done, Ms. Day. I'll come meet you in the Sit Room."

She had to look around to remember where she was—within the circle of Jefferson's knowledge. "I'm not there."

"Where are you?"

Her throat was too dry to answer.

"Shit! You're on site, aren't you? Goddamn it! Get out of there."

Coming from far down the hall she heart the first *blat* of a tuba. Warming up. Not music yet.

Some itch told her that it was too late. That it might be too late to safely evacuate the musicians and the public even now gathering in the Great Hall. Too late to save the library and all of its treasures.

Damien grabbed her arm. His expression said it all.

"Chatter confirms tonight," she told Arnson then hung up the phone.

"How bad?"

Damien didn't shrink under the fear, instead he seemed to grow taller. "Several hundred percent increase in messaging and social media interchanges regarding Shab-e Yalda, but only in the immediate area: DC and Alexandria, Virginia. The rest of the nation is no more active on the subject than usual. They've got four targets of interest and are pushing those out to the proper authorities. You?"

"Sienna, her father, and the Secret Service are all in motion. Sienna will be notifying the President."

"Which means—" Damien was interrupted by another deep *blat* of scales, "—that it may be up to us to solve it."

She grabbed his hand and rushed out of the circle of Jefferson's knowledge, down the exhibition hallway and slammed to a halt against the upper story balustrade that looked down on the Great Hall.

While they had wandered, the area had been transformed. The three white-marble arches at the east end of the Great Hall were now blocked by scores of tubas. A line of forward-facing sousaphones were along the back. In front of them stood dozens more players, clutching standard, bell-upward tubas to their chests. And in front of them another row was seated.

"There are the Marines," Damien pointed.

In the center section, the Marine Corps Band was dressed in brilliantly red, ornate jackets. The men wore dark blue slacks and the women floor-length skirts. Typical.

"Shouldn't they be wearing white hats?" Cornelia was searching for anything that might be out of place.

"Marines never wear their covers, our word for the white hats, indoors unless they're on duty status and wearing a side-arm in which case they want their hands free."

An array of civilian tuba players filled out the spread to either side. They were easy to separate. There were two sections in formal black-and-white attire—those would be the musicians from the symphony and the opera. Then there was a much less formal and larger group, who appeared to be wearing a variety of high school colors. A wide array of musicians, but nothing stood out.

The audience was a much more difficult problem. They were packed in around the base of the tree, ranging up the marble stairs, and now filtering along the mezzanine's balcony rails until they were close enough that she lowered her voice to Damien so as not to be overheard.

"Can we evacuate them?"

He shook his head. "Even if we tried, we'd be sure to create a panic that would get several people injured or killed. And we don't know when."

"Beginning or end of the concert would be my best guess."

"Beginning, that's when I'd do it." Damien's flat statement made Cornelia glad she had *not* been in the military. He'd clearly been trained to consider such matters for best tactics.

"Is there a bomber?"

"Yes and no. To actually damage the building or the collection, it would be more than a man could wear. It would have to be *much* bigger to do more than kill people. But I'd wager that he's here to make sure it goes off."

"Where then?"

"Well, the Christmas tree is hollow. It's built around a steel core. What you're seeing is branches stuck onto the framework."

"Magic."

He nodded in chagrin. "Yes, that's how they get it in here. But I was here when they were setting it up—I do that every year—and I saw nothing unusual. It doesn't have a door in it. They build it from the bottom up and cap it from one of those lifts. They have to take it apart the same way."

Several tubists nodded at each other and then began to run scales together. The deep notes were liquid and flowed upward. Soon the entire orchestra was warming up with scales and exercises. The hall rang with the basso cacophony.

Still Cornelia couldn't see any break in the pattern... unless the break wasn't here.

"Where would their tuba cases be?" They shouted at each other in unison.

Damien pointed. Across the hall, down the stairs, and out a side corridor. "Meeting rooms!" His shout barely reached her though their shoulders were touching due to the press of the growing crowd on either side.

She didn't need his shove to get moving. They raced around the mezzanine. Thankfully the crowds were glued to the balustrade to look down on the concert.

Getting down the stairs was a different matter. A dozen feet wide with a brass handrail up the middle, it was a solid mass of people heading toward them.

Damien took the lead and forced a path downward.

She did her best to shout an apology to the offended as they moved.

The base of the stairs turned and fanned out into the main hall. Those last ten steps were a solid mass of humanity.

She despaired of finding a way through them.

The sound was a palpable force against them. The tuning instruments were breaking into snatches of carols. The crowd was alive with excitement.

They were running out of time, and options.

———

"THERE!" DAMIEN FOUGHT HIS WAY TO THE OUTSIDE BANISTER and glanced over the banister to where an arch opened away from the main floor. Empty. A ten-foot drop.

"Climb up then give me your hands," he didn't give Cornelia a choice. Wrapping his hands about her waist, he lofted her up until her feet were over the banister and she was sitting on it. Then he shifted to grab her hands and used his hip to nudge her butt off the edge.

The yank on her arms must have hurt, but if she cried out in complaint he couldn't hear it. Wouldn't hear a scream of agony in all this racket.

He dangled her as low as he could, then let her go.

She landed clean, ten feet below.

He swung over, catching himself for a moment with his hands on the banister, then dropped down beside her.

They rushed down the side hall toward the meeting rooms.

The first room was crammed with tuba cases. At least the sound reverberating about the Great Hall was far enough away now that he could hear himself think.

He began shaking one case after another.

Empty.

Empty.

Empty.

Cornelia kicked at the first in a long row of them.

It fell and tumbled into the next. Like dominos, a whole line of them went down knocking one after another down. More importantly all of them fell as if they were empty.

He did the same to a row in front of him.

Nothing.

"Next room!" They raced back into the hallway and into the next room.

More cases, each the size of a man's torso.

He tumbled them about, knocking them over and mixing them together. There were going to be some very upset tuba players at the end of the concert. Cornelia didn't have any better luck.

In the next room were the Marine Corps Band's cases, each clearly labeled.

He hated to do it, but he kicked at the stack. They all tumbled aside.

"Maybe we were wrong."

He turned to Cornelia who was working her way down the other side of the room. The Marine Corp Band used rolling road cases for the sousaphones because they traveled so widely. Each was three feet wide, two deep, and almost four high with aluminum corners and heavy latches.

She bumped and nudged her way along them, knocking their metal corners against the walls and leaving scuffs and dings in the wood.

He was about to tell her to ease off when she practically bounced off one that barely moved.

"Check the rest of them," he instructed as he moved in.

When he nudged the case, it moved, but it was very heavy—far heavier than a sousaphone could ever be.

"The rest are empty," she called from the end of the row.

"How long to the bomb squad?"

———

"I'll find out," Cornelia pulled her phone, dialed the general and connected immediately. "We found a case, much heavier than it should be, in the meeting room off the west side of the Great Hall. Bomb, a nuke, an incendiary—we don't know."

"Roger that."

As the general told her that help was about to enter the front of the building, she turned to face back toward Damien.

He was hunched over the case, inspecting it carefully.

Close behind him, a Marine Corps band member stood frozen in the doorway.

She saw everything in a gestalt moment.

He wore the trademark blue pants, red jacket—and white hat.

Cover is never worn indoors unless wearing a sidearm.

A glance down. No sidearm. No pistol belt.

Back to his face.

Grim. Angry. Determined.

"Imposter!" She screamed out the warning to Damien as the man dove toward him.

"What the hell?" General Arnson shouted in her ear.

Damien turned far enough that he dodged the worst of the assailant's blow. Still, he was slammed brutally against the case and the wall.

Dazed for a moment, he struggled to his feet.

For lack of any other weapon, the assailant grabbed a folding metal chair.

Cornelia was too far away to get there in time, so she heaved her phone at his face.

Her aim wasn't that good, but when it struck his neck, his momentary flinch was all the opening Damien needed. His fist drove so hard into the man's face, that he let go of the chair. It was a miracle he didn't fall down dead with the force of the blow.

The chair banged off Damien's shoulder as it fell, but not hard enough to do any damage.

With a cry of rage the man managed to deliver a punch to Damien's solar plexus that sent him staggering back against the wall.

As he moved in once more, Cornelia raced toward him to intercept, having no idea what she'd do when she got there.

When she was still three steps away, there was a soft spitting sound and blood erupted from the man's shoulder, spraying a pattern on the wall before he collapsed to the carpet screaming.

Roy Beaumont stood in the doorway holding a handgun with one of those long silencers on it.

"I take it that he's your problem," Roy said as he checked the area out in the hallway and then looked back into the room.

"Not really," Damien groaned though he still leaned with his back against the wall, gasping for air. "This is," he pointed at the sousaphone case.

"Excuse me?"

"If this is all plastique," Damien knelt down with a knee in the middle of the downed man's back who cried out again. "This could hold...let's see. Half kilo per M112 demolition block? A thousand blocks easy. Call it a half ton. At least this end of the building would probably be destroyed. If it's something worse than C-4..." he shrugged.

Two more Secret Service agents rushed into the room and took charge of the prisoner.

The distant sound of the impending concert caught Cornelia's attention. She snagged her phone from the floor and looked at the time.

"Whatever it is, I think we have less than eight minutes to deal with it."

Then she thought she heard a tiny voice coming from the phone and she put it to her ear.

"Hello?"

"Ms. Day," the general called out, "are you okay?"

"We're fine, except for a bomb that will probably destroy the Library in less than ten minutes."

And then she heard it, in the background, but clear. A sound she knew because she had flown in his helicopter just three long weeks ago.

"Where are you?"

"About a minute out. I didn't know if you'd need air assets, but I went aloft in case you did."

"Damien?"

"Huh?" He looked up from where the two Secret Service agents were binding the assailant's wounds none too gently. He was refusing to speak or make any sound. He appeared ready to go to his heaven along with the bomb. She wasn't having anything to do with that.

"How do we get this out of here?"

"I'm not sure it's even safe to move."

"Well, the bomb squad is going to get here just in time to die with the rest of us. Sitting still isn't an option. Besides, we've already moved it some."

He looked around as if searching his memory with his eyes. "There's a wheelchair ramp that way, but it's through the middle of crowds." He scanned further. "Or... Second street, East Entrance."

He jumped up, kicked a half dozen tuba cases out of the way and began shoving against the rolling sousaphone case.

"You heard?" Cornelia shouted into the phone.

"Meet you there," the general concurred.

She stuffed the phone in her pocket and called for Roy's help. She ran to get the door and they raced down the hall.

———

DAMIEN COULDN'T SEEM TO GET HIS WIND.

The man had been a trained fighter and his massive blow had driven all the air out of Damien's lungs and maybe cracked a few ribs.

The other thing that took his breath away was Cornelia. She hadn't flinched. Not from the moment of her timely warning until she'd rushed bare-handed at an assailant five times her strength. Now she raced ahead of them opening doors as she went.

When one was locked, with a keypad code beside it, she stepped aside and waved them on.

Out of options, he and Roy used the still-rolling mass of the bomb case as a battering ram and blew the door off its lock, practically off its hinges. He'd closed his eyes at the moment of impact, but was still alive to reopen them a moment later. A good indicator that it was C-4 wired to a timer—the stuff was incredibly stable until it was fired off. But with the chance of a booby trap on opening the case, going after the timer itself would be too risky.

They got the case rolling fast enough that Cornelia had to sprint to keep ahead of them. She was a whirlwind: flashing on lights, shoving aside chairs, flipping a folding table aside where it had been set up for some talk.

No time to admire the stunning architecture this time as they raced through. He didn't even dare take a moment to look at his watch. Far behind them, the concert about to begin, the fading sounds becoming more coherent.

At the northeast corner of the building, they almost ran

the case into the Children's Literature Center where the hall took a ninety-degree turn. It was only with a hard scramble that they managed to make the corner and roll the case toward the East Entrance, the one away from all of the people.

They made it down the wheelchair ramp and hit the street at the same moment as the helicopter. It was a Bell helicopter, but a different one. This was a UH-1 Huey, the warhorse of the Vietnam era.

"Good choice," he shouted at the general as they rolled up to it. "I think this is too heavy for the one we took to New York."

The general yanked open a side door and they rolled the case up to it. But even with all four of them grunting against it, they couldn't tip it up into the helicopter's bay.

"Six minutes," Cornelia called out.

"Shit!" Damien looked down at the landing skid he'd been stumbling on while trying to get good footing for the lift. "How strong is that?"

General Arnson looked down at the skid, then nodded. "Strong enough."

In less than a minute they had one set of wheels hopped over the skid and a length of sturdy cable running around the case and tied off inside the cargo bay.

"That's too far off center. I need counterweights if I'm going to fly this damn thing. All aboard and stay up against the far side, as far from the case as you can."

He and Roy scrambled aboard. Staying away from that damn thing wasn't a problem.

Then Cornelia started to follow them.

"Hey! You can't—"

"Don't be an idiot, Damien," she shoved past his protest and they headed aloft.

And she was right. She'd been in as much danger all along as he had. And he'd never find a braver woman than the one now huddled beside him.

Somewhere along the way, they'd lost their coats and the wind roaring past the open cargo bay door sucked the warmth out of them.

Cornelia had yanked on a headset and was talking to the general. He couldn't spot another headset, so he only heard her half of the conversation.

"Four minutes. And that's only if I'm right about the timing."

...

"Yes, it could be less, but then we'll be dead anyway."

...

"No, we don't know what kind of bomb it is."

...

"Well, if we're wrong and it doesn't go off, they can always send a team down to figure it out later."

...

"If we can get there in time, we could drop it at—"

...

"Exactly."

The general must have had the same idea she did and said it the moment before she could. This wasn't the time to ask what they were thinking.

"Two minutes. Get ready!" She shouted to him and Roy.

He nodded. Every second they got it further away from Washington, DC the better. If it was nuclear, there would be no way to save themselves no matter how fast they flew. Best to use every second to save the city.

For half a second he hoped that Cornelia hadn't figured that out, then he laughed.

"What?" she shouted at him.

He swung her boom microphone out of the way and dragged her in to kiss her and kiss her hard.

Of course she'd known that. She'd probably figured it out before he had. Probably before she'd forced her way onto the helicopter. And yet she'd come anyway. Knowing she could have been safe, Cornelia Day had to see it through to the end.

"I love you," he shouted at her.

She nodded. Then her eyes unfocused for a moment as she listened.

She nodded her head and shouted, "Got it!" not realizing that her mic boom was still swung out of the way and the general wouldn't hear her in the cockpit.

That's one on you, Cornelia.

"Let it go!"

Damien yanked the knot loose and the case began tipping away.

Roy slid across the sloped deck plating and planted a boot on it to hurry it on its way. It seemed to take forever to finally lean away and slowly fall off the skid. But once it did, it plummeted downward.

It was probably a stupid thing to do, but all three of them huddled in the chill of the open cargo doorway and watched the case as it tumbled down out of the sky. The general brought the aircraft to a hover well to the side and turned on a searchlight to follow it down.

Down into the Potomac. It was perfect. Between Cornelia and General Arnson, they'd decided to dump the case into the Potomac, it would at least buffer the explosion.

The splashdown sent a plume of spray aloft.

They waited and waited. It was the longest minute of his life.

"Maybe the fall destroyed the mechanism and it—"

A shaft of foaming water exploded upward. It rose well over a hundred feet high and twice as wide at the center of a mile-wide stretch of the river.

It wasn't nuclear, or they'd be dead by now, but it was one damn big hole in the water.

He reached out to close the cargo bay door. As he did, he saw exactly where they were. Damien could only shake his head.

The Marine Corps at Quantico were going to have some explaining to do tomorrow about why they were detonating high explosives where a civilian river ran so close beside their own base.

13

Only by lack of a bridesmaid dress had Cornelia been able to beg off from becoming a member of Sienna's and Roy's State Dining Room wedding on the first floor of the Residence.

"Besides," Cornelia had told her, "I'm nearly a foot taller than you are. I'd look ridiculous."

"No, only half a foot, and you'd look lovely. Besides, are you saying that I'll look ridiculous when I'm bridesmaid at your wedding?"

That was no longer as uncomfortable a thought as it had been.

"I'll make sure there's time for all of us to get dresses," she retreated to her earlier excuse and Sienna was too happy to protest Cornelia's escape.

The three days after the explosion had been incredibly busy, even by her new standards.

Debriefing, closing the files, and sending a very back-channel thank you to President Madani and his son-in-law had occupied the first day. She'd sent them Katz's largest gift basket, with no card, delivered by Swiss Diplomatic pouch.

The second day had been the aftermath: twelve more arrests of three different bomb makers, that had then branched out into materiel providers. That was the only part of the entire operation to receive any news coverage: *Arrest of suspected terrorists.*

On the morning of Christmas Eve, an answer had come back from President Madani in the form of a beautiful, hand-illuminated copy of the love poems by the ancient Sufi poet Hafez. He had inscribed it with: "C.D., This is my favorite translation. Please share it only with a man filled with the common sense to appreciate you, J.M."

"New world meets the old world, pastrami and poetry," Damien had joked, but he'd handled the book as reverently as she had.

Christmas Eve evening itself had been a very quiet, very loving night at his apartment. He'd served her a roast beef and Yorkshire pudding picnic—spread on the carpet before a small but colorful Christmas tree.

Damien had proven his ability to cook a wonderful meal and she had proven her complete inability to be of much help.

They'd laughed together through *When Harry Met Sally,* but there was nothing fake about what happened between them later that night.

She'd found a copy of *Landmarks* for him and he'd given her *The Gatekeeper.*

"Missy LeHand was called FDR's personal secretary. You may be the first woman to bear the title, but she was really the first female Chief of Staff. Hell of a legacy you've stepped into. I can't think of a woman more capable of doing it."

The way Damien saw her never ceased to amaze her.

The Christmas Day wedding party itself had grown all out of hand. According to Sienna, she still had no idea how it had happened and Cornelia had better be careful or it would happen to her.

The out-going President and First Lady had insisted that Sienna and Roy hold their wedding in the Residence. Members of the Cabinet, the entire Joint Chiefs of Staff, and a small phalanx of Roy's Secret Service friends had joined in, as well as all of the senior staff.

Cornelia's own inclusion in the immediate wedding party, if not the ceremony itself, had been a foregone conclusion. She, Anne, Alice, and Geneviève had gathered about Sienna. Wine and merriment had flowed thickly among them.

"No wine for me," Anne had declared.

Without hesitation, Genny had squealed more like a little girl than a dignified First Lady. "There will be another baby in the White House! Yes, this is perfection."

That had only wound the group up even more until everyone who came near looked at them as if they were more than a little bit crazy.

The fever had continued to build until the ceremony, leaving Cornelia feeling positively giddy.

Or so she'd thought until the arrival of the wedding processional itself. Damien had not managed to escape being co-opted into the ceremony. Actually, he'd seemed positively delighted by the idea, though he'd declined to explain why.

The State Dining Room had been the center of the Christmas madness—before the wedding was added to it. The four corners of the room were commanded by towering white-flocked trees adorned with silvered balls that captured and reflected every light.

The walls were draped in silver and gold garlands and the ceiling had so many icicle lights that they might have been inside an ice cave. There wasn't a hint of chill, however. The great carpet of the State Dining Room had been rolled up to reveal the rich warmth of white oak herringbone parquet beneath.

Across its surface, rose petals were scattered by the three-year-old Adele—coaxed along by her tall and lovely nanny, herself the adopted daughter of a Hostage Rescue Team sniper.

Then behind the bridesmaids, who'd winked at her as they paced by, came an honor guard made up of White House Marines.

Cornelia supposed it was only fitting. The father of the bride, Marine Corps General Edward Arnson, had *very* recently been promoted from a one-star brigadier to a two-star major general for his long service—and unspecified heroism in flight.

Then, lastly before the bride and her two-star escort, came a lone Marine.

At first Cornelia didn't recognize him.

Damien always looked good to her. But in his dress uniform—complete with side-arm and Mameluke sword, and wearing his white cover—he was about the handsomest man she'd ever seen.

The man who wanted to protect her, but who hadn't shut her out either. Together they had saved the Christmas season, and the words and spirit of their country. Together they had saved *her* words.

His face was perfectly passive as he did his formal march up the aisle—sword at the ready, unsheathed and held close by his shoulder. No one would be stupid enough to challenge the couple at the altar with Damien standing guard.

And then she noticed the one tiny thing that was out of place.

Captain Damien Feinman didn't wear a captain's bars on the shoulder boards of his uniform, but rather a major's oak leaf. At her gasp, she saw the tiniest smile touch his lips before he passed her by.

And later that evening, when the ceremony was done and the cake had been eaten, after the dancing had wound down and most of the guests had left, Damien came to her. Close by his side stood General Arnson, still in his full dress uniform. And with him Zachary, Daniel, and President Matthews.

"Why doesn't this look good?" It wasn't fair that there was some crisis at a wedding on Christmas Day. She needed one day without a disaster.

Damien did one of those immaculate moves that Marines did, handing off his cover to the general who accepted it with formality.

Damien turned back to her, and then dropped to one knee.

Cornelia forgot how to breathe in that moment.

He took her hand and looked up at her.

"Please say yes, Cornelia Day. I am a man of too many words—"

"You've got that right," the general agreed in a gruff tone that cracked a smile on Damien's upturned face.

"So I will keep this simple. I said I wouldn't propose before New Years Day, but I can't wait that long. There is no future I want without you in it every single day. Please say yes."

"He did it okay," Zachary said to Daniel.

"Better than I did."

"You did great," Alice came up beside him. "Though I

wouldn't have minded if you'd been wearing a spiffy uniform like that one when you proposed."

Anne slipped beside Zachary and moved up against him. He tucked her beneath his arm and it was about the best recommendation Cornelia had ever seen for a happy couple.

"Did we miss it?" Sienna rushed up with Roy in tow. "Please tell me we didn't miss it. This is the good part."

Roy kissed the top of her head, "The good part is only starting, my wife. You'll see."

"Shush, all of you. You haven't given this poor girl a chance to speak." Nobody appeared ready to argue with the First Lady.

Cornelia tried to speak, she really did. But nothing came out.

All of these people, these wonderful couples, were hovering, waiting for her to be as happy as they were.

And kneeling at her feet, a man she loved for his wit, his wisdom, and his bravery. He wasn't just handsome, he was also beautiful.

Unable to find the words, she knelt down in front of him and simply nodded.

Reaching into his pocket, he pulled out a ring. A simple diamond in a smoothly elegant band. No deep symbolism. No scribed words. Simple truth.

As he slipped it on her finger, the joy inside was so great that she still couldn't speak.

But somewhere she found the laugh that had always been locked away deep inside her. So she wrapped her arms around him and they laughed together as their friends joined them.

———

If you enjoyed this book,
please consider leaving a review.
They really help.
Damien's Christmas

Keep reading for an exciting excerpt from:
Night Stalkers Holiday #8:
Christmas at Peleliu Cove

THE NIGHT STALKERS HOLIDAY #8 (EXCERPT)

IF YOU ENJOYED THAT, DIVE INTO…

CHRISTMAS AT PELELIU COVE
(EXCERPT)

Striding up the wide bow ramp of the LCAC hovercraft, Petty Officer Nika Maier patted the ugly beast on its big black numbers—316—painted on the Navy-gray hull.

"Morning, baby." It was 1800 hours, an hour past sunset in the southern Mediterranean, the start of their day. Ever since the Night Stalkers had come to fly helicopters off their ship, operations had been done in a flipped-clock world of the night. Even in their second year aboard, she really wasn't used to sleeping through the day, but that choice was made way above the pay grade of a Navy enlisted.

Despite the warm December evening, there was a familiar damp air-and-steel chill down in the bowels of the USS *Peleliu* where Landing Craft Air Cushion 316 was typically parked.

"You got a soft spot in you," Senior Chief Petty Officer Sly Stowell's deep voice echoed about the steel cavern that was the sea-level Well Deck of the ship. The *Peleliu's* massive stern ramp was currently raised, blocking out both the sea and the last of the sunset. In the shadows of the worklights she hadn't spotted him. The Craftmaster was perched in the window of the hovercraft's starboard two-story control station, but after four tours in the Navy, she'd lost her ability to be surprised and simply waved a greeting.

"Only before a mission," she looked up at him. "Other than that..."

"...hard as steel," he finished for her. "In a mood to go kick some ass, Petty Officer Maier?" He offered his ritual start-of-shift greeting.

"Two boots better than one, Senior Stowell," her ritual reply before she climbed up into her Loadmaster's portside tower to prep the hovercraft. Even on days with no mission or exercise planned, they always made sure their craft was completely ready.

Sly dropped down the ladder and headed off to the evening briefing as she started checking over the LCAC—spoken like you were about to throw up—El-Cack! Some part of her warped Lower East Side Jewish sense of humor laughed every single time she heard it...or even thought it. The LCAC was homely as a Bowery bum, and so powerful that riding in it felt like an outing in the Lord's personal chariot. The juxtaposition got her every time. Probably made her completely sophomoric, but since no one could hear inside her head she figured no harm—no foul.

The portside lookout on Sly Stowell's hovercraft had become Petty Officer Nika Maier's favorite assignment since joining the Navy eight years before. In just another month she'd have been four years on old Lady 316.

Her first tour had been aboard the USS *George H. W. Bush*—that was then on its own first cruise—but a girl could get lost in the five-thousand-person city that was then a newly commissioned aircraft carrier. The largest ship afloat in any navy, and still the crowd was worse than Times Square on New Year's Eve. She'd been a *red*—a red-vested serviceperson—in charge of loading and securing aircraft weapons and munitions systems.

She was no aviator, but eventually grew sick of watching others burn into the sky on the hottest rides while she stood on the deck, ate exhaust fumes, and wished she was someone else.

For a brief time, a very brief time, the length of a two-week training run, she'd switched over to a Cyclone-class patrol boat without an aircraft in sight—not even a helipad. The hundred-and-eighty-foot boat slipped in close to the action, mostly on security patrols for bigger ships. She'd enjoyed that. And the weapon systems were exceptional—there were six major weapon systems on a boat commonly crewed by thirty men and women.

But that was the catch. On the USS *Firebolt*, a girl *couldn't* get lost. With such a small crew, the pickings were painfully thin for friendships, never mind any other, more personal types of ships. And the *Firebolt's* grapevine news network offered no privacy at all—she couldn't switch from drinking iced tea to lemonade at lunch without raising comments and questions. Good people, but way too far into her life.

Nika's Loadmaster checklist on the LCAC was short until they had a load. It was still fifteen minutes to start of shift, so she grabbed Jerome's checklist and began the mechanical inspection. She was the only one other than Sly who had cross-trained in all five of the crew positions; but it required constant practice to keep her skills fresh.

Step One: Perimeter inspection. She headed down the bow ramp and began working her way along the spray skirt looking for untoward damage. The vague slit of light coming in over the *Peleliu's* rear ramp was no help at all, but the big worklights shone down. She pulled a flashlight out of her thigh pocket to double-check in the shadows cast by the overheads.

This, her third ship—three hundred feet shorter and half the personnel of the super carrier—landed right in the sweet spot. The USS *Peleliu* had serviced a Marine Expeditionary Unit for thirty-five years. Cobra helicopters and Harrier jets up on the flattop deck. Beneath that and the Hanger Deck were several decks carrying eighteen hundred gung-ho Marines and close to a thousand Navy to run the eight-hundred-foot ship and keep the Marines out of trouble in between when they went out to fight it.

Even though Nika had liked the size, she'd still felt disconnected. Most of her second tour had gone by and she'd been doubting the point of re-upping for a third. Dropping down into the reserves or National Guard and having a civilian life hadn't exactly thrilled her either.

Then, four years ago, Sly had introduced her to heaven. She patted her baby-girl 316 again as she inspected the rear ramp gasket seal. She remembered the day with crystal clarity—

It had been midday and the Indian Ocean heat had dehydrated her to the point of weaving, weighed down by her bright red fire-resistant gear. She'd just left the Flight Deck after double-checking the Zuni missile control connections on yet another SuperCobra helicopter when Senior Chief Petty Officer Sly Stowell had pulled her aside.

Everyone knew Sly, he was just one of *those* guys. Super competent. There were days it seemed the *Peleliu* would sink without him aboard. Other times people said that they didn't need a command structure as long as Sly was around.

"You look bored as hammered shit, Maier," were the first words he'd ever spoken directly to her. She hadn't realized that he even knew her name.

Sometimes a girl answered honesty with honesty.

"Damn straight, Senior. If I never have to load another hang another Hellfire, stare down another Hydra 70 missile tube, or fuck with another buggered up bomb mount, I'll die a happy woman."

"Good, come with me," and he'd walked away from her.

At a loss for what else to do, she'd grabbed a water bottle and staggered after him.

He'd led her down past the personnel decks. And then on down, below the on-board Garage Decks filled with tanks, Humvees, and a dozen different land and amphibious vehicles. The drivers used the roof hatches to get in and out of them once they were parked because they were jammed into the ship's lower holds door-to-door.

He led her down to the Well Deck. She hadn't been down here but once or twice since her on-boarding orientation tour earlier in the year. The air had been oddly fresher down below than up on the burning plain of the Flight Deck, and thanks be to the Lord our God.

Right at sea-level, the *Peleliu* sported a massive stern gate. When lowered into the water it formed an angled steel beach, opening the Well Deck directly to the sea. A variety of landing craft could be parked there.

"Meet my baby," Sly had sounded like a proud papa despite being from North Carolina rather than a good Jewish family. Or even a bad one like hers.

It was an LCAC, about the ugliest sea craft ever built. No surprise that they named the craft so that it sounded like a cat choking up a hairball. Worse, its only name was the black numbers painted as tall as Nika's torso. Aircraft, ships, even sailboats had names; El-Cacks didn't even rate that.

She'd studied the LCAC. A Landing Craft Air Cushion was a ninety-foot-long by fifty-foot-wide rectangular box with no lid and four jet engines down the sides—combined, they packed the same shaft horsepower as a Boeing 737 airliner. They powered two huge fans at the stern and two more that drove air underneath her big rubber skirt. There was a two-story control station at the starboard front corner for three people and a smaller tower for some loner to port. After the mayhem of the Flight Deck, that isolated tower had looked attractive.

At the base of either tower was a narrow cabin for a total of thirty troops. Down the center was an open deck that could hold an M1A1 Abrams Main Battle Tank or a dozen armored Humvees parked in three tight lanes.

Even on that first day aboard four years ago, she'd felt a strange affinity for the poor beast of a machine. Neither boat nor aircraft, the hovercraft lay there on the Well Deck like a stuck pig with her rubber skirt deflated and the front and rear ramps laying open on the rough wood of the dry Well Deck. The LCAC looked like a cross between a sad puppy and a giant steel shoebox someone had slashed the corners on and pushed the end flaps down.

She'd known that high above, the Flight Deck would still be awash in the burning daylight glow and fresh sea air —liberally laced with the kerosene bite of fresh-burned Jet-A fuel and echoing with the roar of turboshaft engines.

The bowels of the ship were dark and quiet except for the beat of the sea against the outside of the hull and the low thrum of the big steam turbines directly below—more felt through the heels of her boots than heard.

With the *Peleliu's* stern gate up, only a narrow slice of light had entered above the gate. Big worklights did little to chase away the shadowed cave that was the Well Deck. It was like a man-cave on steroids—without the bar and big-screen television.

"Ain't she a beauty?" Sly had asked in his lazy Southern drawl, which echoed about the vast compartment like a whisper in Temple Emanu-El, the massive synagogue that her mother always dragged her to for the high holidays. As if showing up ten times a year somehow made them Upper East Side New York Jews rather than the last of the Lower East Side holdouts against encroaching Chinatown. Encroaching, hell. The Chinese had overrun the old Jewish neighborhood and most of Little Italy. But the Maiers would not be nudged loose from their appointed place in the world.

Thankfully Sly hadn't waited for her to answer.

"She needs a crew of five to fly and I just lost my portside spotter and Loadmaster," he aimed a nod up at the slim one-person tower that she'd liked on first sight. "Something about falling in love with an accountant, wants kids. You want kids, Maier?"

"Not yet, Senior. Haven't found a man worth having them with."

"Good. You already have your boatswain's rating. Welcome aboard."

———

Buy now to keep reading at fine retailers everywhere:
Christmas at Peleliu Cove
And please consider leaving a review, they really help.
Damien's Christmas

ABOUT THE AUTHOR

USA Today and Amazon #1 Bestseller M. L. "Matt" Buchman began writing on a flight from Japan to ride his bicycle across the Australian Outback. Just part of a solo around-the-world trip that ultimately launched his writing career.

From the very beginning, his powerful female heroines insisted on putting character first, *then* a great adventure. He's since written over 70 action-adventure thrillers and military romantic suspense novels. And just for the fun of it: 100 short stories, and a fast-growing pile of read-by-author audiobooks.

Booklist says: "3X Top 10 of the Year." PW says: "Tom Clancy fans open to a strong female lead will clamor for more." His fans say: "I want more now...of everything." That his characters are even more insistent than his fans is a hoot.

As a 30-year project manager with a geophysics degree who has designed and built houses, flown and jumped out of planes, and solo-sailed a 50' ketch, he is awed by what is possible. More at: www.mlbuchman.com.

Other works by M. L. Buchman: *(* - also in audio)*

Action-Adventure Thrillers

Dead Chef
One Chef!
Two Chef!

Miranda Chase
Drone*
Thunderbolt*
Condor*
Ghostrider*
Raider*
Chinook*
Havoc*
White Top*
Start the Chase*

Science Fiction / Fantasy

Deities Anonymous
Cookbook from Hell: Reheated
Saviors 101

Single Titles
Monk's Maze
the Me and Elsie Chronicles

Contemporary Romance

Eagle Cove
Return to Eagle Cove
Recipe for Eagle Cove
Longing for Eagle Cove
Keepsake for Eagle Cove

Love Abroad
Heart of the Cotswolds: England
Path of Love: Cinque Terre, Italy

Where Dreams
Where Dreams are Born
Where Dreams Reside
Where Dreams Are of Christmas*
Where Dreams Unfold
Where Dreams Are Written
Where Dreams Continue

Non-Fiction

Strategies for Success
Managing Your Inner Artist/Writer
Estate Planning for Authors*
Character Voice
Narrate and Record Your Own
Audiobook*

Short Story Series by M. L. Buchman:

Action-Adventure Thrillers

Dead Chef

Miranda Chase Origin Stories

Romantic Suspense

Antarctic Ice Fliers

US Coast Guard

Contemporary Romance

Eagle Cove

Other

Deities Anonymous (fantasy)

Single Titles

The Emily Beale Universe
(military romantic suspense)

The Night Stalkers
MAIN FLIGHT
The Night Is Mine
I Own the Dawn
Wait Until Dark
Take Over at Midnight
Light Up the Night
Bring On the Dusk
By Break of Day
Target of the Heart
Target Lock on Love
Target of Mine
Target of One's Own
NIGHT STALKERS HOLIDAYS
*Daniel's Christmas**
*Frank's Independence Day**
*Peter's Christmas**
Christmas at Steel Beach
*Zachary's Christmas**
*Roy's Independence Day**
*Damien's Christmas**
Christmas at Peleliu Cove

Henderson's Ranch
*Nathan's Big Sky**
*Big Sky, Loyal Heart**
*Big Sky Dog Whisperer**
*Tales of Henderson's Ranch**

Shadow Force: Psi
*At the Slightest Sound**
*At the Quietest Word**
*At the Merest Glance**
*At the Clearest Sensation**

White House Protection Force
*Off the Leash**
*On Your Mark**
*In the Weeds**

Firehawks
Pure Heat
Full Blaze
*Hot Point**
*Flash of Fire**
Wild Fire
SMOKEJUMPERS
*Wildfire at Dawn**
*Wildfire at Larch Creek**
*Wildfire on the Skagit**

Delta Force
*Target Engaged**
*Heart Strike**
*Wild Justice**
*Midnight Trust**

Emily Beale Universe Short Story Series
The Night Stalkers
The Night Stalkers Stories
The Night Stalkers CSAR
The Night Stalkers Wedding Stories
The Future Night Stalkers

Delta Force
Th Delta Force Shooters
The Delta Force Warriors

Firehawks
The Firehawks Lookouts
The Firehawks Hotshots
The Firebirds

White House Protection Force
Stories

Future Night Stalkers
Stories (Science Fiction)

The Emily Beale Universe
Reading Order Road Map

any series and any novel may be read stand-alone
(all have a complete heartwarming Happy Ever After)

The Emily Beale Universe

The Night Stalkers
(#1 *The Night Is Mine*)

The Night Stalkers
5D, 5E & CSAR
Stories

Night Stalkers
Holidays

Delta Force

Firehawks

Henderson's
Ranch

Delta Force
Stories

Smokejumpers

White House
Protection Force

ShadowForce
PSI

Fire Lookouts,
Hotshots,
& Firebirds
Stories

Dilya's
Dog Force*

WHPF
Stories

The Future
Night Stalkers
Stories

* Coming soon

For more information and alternate reading orders, please
visit: www.mlbuchman.com/reading-order

SIGN UP FOR M. L. BUCHMAN'S NEWSLETTER TODAY

and receive:
Release News
Free Short Stories
a Free Book

Get your free book today. Do it now.
free-book.mlbuchman.com

www.ingramcontent.com/pod-product-compliance
Lightning Source LLC
Chambersburg PA
CBHW020632110726
47899CB00002B/743